Luigi compressed his lips. "We have unfinished business."

"That was a mistake," retorted Megan on a loud whisper.

"Like marrying me was a mistake?" He couldn't help himself. He'd been so confident that tonight was the night they'd both realize that they couldn't sleep apart, and to have it all snatched away from him because Charlotte had had a bad dream drove him crazy.

"Since you put it like that, yes." Her eyes were cool on his, her earlier passion gone.

"I think you're lying," he said. "You're afraid to admit it, but you still care for me."

"In your dreams," she hissed.

"Then why, when I kiss you, do you melt in my arms? Why do you return my kiss with so much passion that it makes a lie of everything you're saying? Tell me that, dear wife of mine. Look me in the eye and tell me you have no feelings for me."

MARRIAGE AND MISTLETOE

When millionaires claim Christmas brides...

Snow is falling, lights are sparkling,
the scene is set—for winter seductions and
festive white weddings!

Don't miss any of our exciting stories this
month in Promotional Harlequin Presents!
Available now, in December 2007:

The Rancher's Rules
Lucy Monroe

Her Husband's Christmas Bargain
Margaret Mayo

The Christmas Night Miracle
Carole Mortimer

The Italian Tycoon's Bride
Helen Brooks

HER HUSBAND'S CHRISTMAS BARGAIN

MARGARET MAYO

MARRIAGE AND MISTLETOE

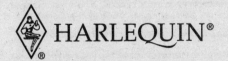

HARLEQUIN®

TORONTO • NEW YORK • LONDON
AMSTERDAM • PARIS • SYDNEY • HAMBURG
STOCKHOLM • ATHENS • TOKYO • MILAN • MADRID
PRAGUE • WARSAW • BUDAPEST • AUCKLAND

ISBN-13: 978-0-373-82058-0
ISBN-10:   0-373-82058-5

HER HUSBAND'S CHRISTMAS BARGAIN

First North American Publication 2007.

Copyright © 2004 by Margaret Mayo.

www.eHarlequin.com

Printed in U.S.A.

MARGARET MAYO is a hopeless romantic who loves writing and falls in love with every one of her heroes. It was never her ambition to become an author, although she always loved reading, even to the extent of reading comics out loud to her twin brother when she was eight years old.

She was born in Staffordshire, England, and has lived in the same part of the country ever since. She left school to become a secretary, taking a break to have her two children, Adrian and Tina. Once they were at school she started back to work and planned to further her career by becoming a bilingual secretary. Unfortunately she couldn't speak any languages other than her native English, so she began evening classes. It was at this time that she got the idea for a romantic short story. Margaret, and her mother before her, had always read Mills & Boon romances, and to actually be writing one excited her beyond measure. She forgot the languages and now has over seventy novels to her credit.

Before she became a successful author Margaret was extremely shy and found it difficult to talk to strangers. For research purposes she forced herself to speak to people from all walks of life and now says her shyness has gone forever—to a certain degree. She is still happier pouring out her thoughts on paper.

CHAPTER ONE

IT WASN'T! It was! It *was* Megan. Luigi Costanzo had over-heard the child telling Santa that all she wanted for Christmas was a daddy. It had aroused his curiosity, even caused a faint stir somewhere deep within him, and he'd watched her as she returned to her mother. She was a pretty little girl with long blonde hair and big blue eyes, but it was the shock of seeing who was her parent that caused him to do a double take.

Megan!

His Megan!

Megan, whom he hadn't seen for almost four years.

What the hell?

Luigi looked from mother to daughter and his eyes narrowed. Megan still had the same shoulder-length blonde hair, the same slender figure; nothing about her had changed. She didn't even look any older. He swung on his heel, snapping his fingers at his nearest employee. 'Please follow that woman and report back to me with her address.'

'Yes, sir.'

If the young man was surprised he didn't show it. He spurted into immediate action. There was no arguing with the new owner of Gerards. He'd had everyone on their toes ever since he took over a few months ago.

* * *

'Sweetheart, what did you ask for?' Megan looked down at her beloved daughter, who was skipping happily along at her side. There hadn't really been time to visit Santa's grotto but Charlotte had pleaded so eloquently that Megan couldn't find it in her heart to refuse. There was always another train, even if it meant travelling home at the height of the rush hour.

'For a daddy.'

Megan hid her surprise, smiling indulgently instead. 'I don't think Santa supplies daddies. You were supposed to ask for a toy.' Her heart felt heavy as she spoke. Charlotte was right, she did need a father, and if Luigi had been different…

Megan halted her thoughts. It was no good letting them run along those lines. She had been an idiot for marrying him, for allowing her parents to convince her that she could do no better. He was a man with big ambition; she would never want for anything, they had said.

She could understand their reasoning because money had been the bane of their lives, her father never able to hold down a job for long due to ill health, so for that reason she hadn't told her parents that she was leaving Luigi. She had simply disappeared, telephoning them later so that they would know she was safe, but not giving them her address. They had not been happy, telling her that she was making a big mistake. But Megan didn't think so.

Luigi's chief aim in life was making money, and he was very good at it. His wife was someone to clean his home, and cook and wash for him, and to make love to whenever the urge drove him. But there was no love in his heart; she had found that out after the first few months of marriage. She doubted he was capable of feeling any such emotion. Whereas she had loved him with a passion that had sometimes scared her.

With an effort she pushed him out of her mind, concentrating instead on her chatterbox daughter. Santa had given her a parcel and they played a guessing game all the way home as to what was inside.

Home was a rented terraced house in Greenwich, which she shared with Jenny Wilson whom she'd met when she first arrived in London. As soon as they were indoors Charlotte ripped the wrapping paper off her gift. If Megan was disappointed her daughter wasn't. She was delighted with her soldier doll.

'Look, Mummy, I can pretend he's my daddy. Wasn't Santa kind?'

It was a clear case of the boys and girls presents getting muddled but Megan hadn't the heart to tell Charlotte this. 'He certainly is, sweetheart. What are you going to call him?'

'Daddy, of course,' said Charlotte scornfully. 'Come on, Daddy, come and play with me.'

It broke Megan's heart to see her daughter being so passionate about a doll. She hadn't realised that Charlotte missed having a father. Where had the idea come from? Surely she was too young to know?

Daddy doll was a part of their lives for the next few days and on Sunday morning, when Charlotte jumped into bed beside her, the doll had to come too. Megan was sometimes tempted to conveniently lose the doll, except that she knew her daughter would be heartbroken. The trouble was, all this talk about Daddy dragged up memories she would far rather forget.

When the doorbell rang loudly and insistently she was tempted to ignore it. This was Sunday morning for heaven's sake. No one of any consequence called at this hour. It was probably for Jenny anyway, and she was spending the weekend with her fiancé. But the ringing didn't stop; whoever it was kept their finger on the button with no intention of going away until it was answered.

Impatiently Megan pulled on her dressing gown. 'Stay there and keep the bed warm,' she told her daughter. Someone was going to get a piece of her mind. But that someone robbed her of speech. She felt the colour drain from her face, and her heart skipped a couple of beats before resuming at a startling pace.

The very last person she had expected to see was her husband. After all these years she had thought she was safe. In fact she'd felt extremely secure in the knowledge that he had no idea where she was. Not that she'd expected him to come looking. He might just as well have employed a housekeeper for all the notice he'd ever taken of her.

He was still as handsome as ever, his dark Latin looks improving with age rather than fading. Black hair aggressively short, deep brown eyes intensely disturbing. There was maybe a line or two around their corners but it added rather than detracted from his appearance. His nose was strong and straight and his generous lips were at this moment compressed into a grim line.

Although there was a step up into her house he still stood a couple of inches taller. He was six three compared to her five feet six and she was glad at this moment of the extra few inches the step afforded her. He could be very intimidating when he chose.

And it looked as though this was one of those occasions.

'I've come to claim my daughter.'

The bald statement left Megan gasping. This was her worst nightmare come true. She clung to the door handle for support as her legs threatened to buckle. 'H—how did you know?' She felt a tightness in her throat that threatened to choke her.

'So she is mine!' he claimed triumphantly, a gleam of light entering those dark, dark eyes.

He had tricked her! Megan felt like taking a swipe at him. Or at the very least slamming the door in his face. But what good would that do? He wouldn't go away until he'd got what he came for. She dared not think what that might be.

'Can I come in or shall we negotiate on the doorstep?'

Negotiate? Negotiate what? Visiting rights? Some hope of that. He was no longer a part of her life, their lives, hers and Charlotte's. She ought to have divorced him. How had he found her? The question whirled round and round in her head.

He lived in Derbyshire; he had no connections with London. She had thought she would be safe a hundred and fifty or more miles away in a big anonymous city. So how had he discovered her whereabouts? Had he been looking for her all these years? Somehow she doubted it. He had declared he loved her before they got married but there had been very little show of affection afterwards, certainly not enough for him to take time off from his precious work to scour the country after her.

He looked as though he'd done well for himself. A short black Crombie overcoat, mohair trousers with perfectly pressed pleats, Italian leather shoes. Yes, he wasn't short of a few pennies. Not that he ever had been. But he was far more polished, far more mature and self-confident. Even the way he stood told her that.

There was not an ounce of diffidence. He was here on a mission and expected to get his own way. No, not expected, he would demand it—as his right. She could see it in his expression. Dark eyes overpowered her, making her step back and invite him silently into her private domain.

She didn't want to do it but she had no choice. He was

hypnotising her into obeying. Or was it because she didn't want to argue with him in full view of her neighbours? Whichever, she was going along with his wishes and she had the secret fear that she would live to regret it.

He followed her as she opened the door into her lounge-cum-dining room, standing just inside the doorway as she drew back the curtains and let the cold morning light filter in. She folded her arms and looked at him as imperiously as she was able in her purple wool dressing gown. It wasn't exactly the outfit she would have chosen for facing the enemy.

And he *was* her enemy if he thought he was going to take Charlotte away from her. The very notion triggered a protective parent syndrome. Her grey eyes flared hostility and her back stiffened. 'How did you find me?'

'Does it matter?' he asked coolly. 'The issue here is that you have denied me my daughter.'

'And you think you'd have made a good father?' Megan's voice was growing shriller by the second. 'You didn't even show *me* any affection; I had no intention of putting a child through that.'

He drew in a swift disbelieving breath. 'I was working for our future, Megan, in case you'd forgotten.'

'So *I* didn't matter?'

'Of course you mattered. But I thought you understood.'

'Oh, I understood all right,' she retorted. 'You thought I'd be happy taking a back seat while you headed towards making your first million. You believed that the thought of all that money would be sufficient for me to happily keep house while you spent every waking hour making more of the bloody stuff. Well, let me tell you something, dear husband of mine, I'm not interested in money. So long as I have enough to put a roof over mine and Charlotte's head and feed and clothe us, then—'

'So that's my daughter's name—Charlotte. Mmm, I like it,' he cut in with a smile. 'Where is she? I'd like to—'

'She's asleep,' lied Megan, 'and I'd thank you to keep your voice down.'

'I want to see her.'

'And then you'll go away?' she rasped. 'I don't think so. I didn't like it when you said you'd come to *claim* your daughter. What was that supposed to mean? Because I'll tell you this right now, it will be over my dead body that you take her from me.'

Megan could hear herself shrieking and knew that it was no way to conduct herself, but she couldn't help it. He wasn't going to take Charlotte; *he wasn't!* She would fight him tooth and nail.

'What I want,' he said, 'is for you and Charlotte to come and spend Christmas with me.'

Megan stared at him in disbelief, finally shaking her head. 'You really think we'd do that? You think I'd let my daughter spend Christmas with a stranger?'

The jibe hurt; she could see it in his eyes, but she didn't care. How dare he think he could walk in here and take over her life?

'I'm not a stranger *I* am her father,' he rasped, 'and as such I have rights. You must know that. And if necessary I'll implement those rights,' he added harshly. 'If you know what's good for you you'll accept that you have no alternative.'

He moved further into the room, halting a few menacing inches from her. Megan felt every hair on her skin prickle and she wanted to step back but she knew that she must show no fear or he would take advantage. Luigi could be ruthless. If he wanted something he went all out for it. She'd seen it enough times in his business life and knew that he'd be equally determined where his daughter was concerned. She was being hounded into a corner and wasn't sure which way to turn.

When his big hands gripped her shoulders she felt a powerful sensation rush through her—anger, fear, desperation. All three! With a strength she didn't know she possessed, Megan pushed him away. Then out of the corner of her eye, she saw Charlotte sidling into the room—a scared-looking Charlotte.

'Mummy,' her daughter cried plaintively. 'What's that man doing to you?'

Megan immediately gathered the child into her arms. 'Nothing, sweetheart.'

'But I saw him touch you. Were you fighting?'

'Of course not.'

'So who is he? What's he doing here?'

Megan could understand Charlotte's questions because they never had any male visitors except Jenny's boyfriend. There'd been no one in her life since Luigi, not because she'd been short of invitations; she simply wasn't interested. Her daughter filled her every waking hour and Megan was completely happy—or she had been until a few minutes ago. Now she felt her happiness fading and worry begin to take its place.

It was ironic that Luigi should put in an appearance now—when Charlotte was crying out for a daddy. He had unknowingly timed his visit to perfection. And it looked as though he intended to do all in his power to take her beloved baby away from her. It was as clear in her head as water out of a tap that this was what he had in mind. He didn't want her, he wanted Charlotte.

I've come to claim my daughter!

Those were his exact words and they struck chill in her heart as she recalled them. And because of that how could she explain to Charlotte that this was her father? He had no part to play in their lives. Not now, not ever! But how was she to get rid of him?

'It looks as though Mummy isn't going to tell you who I am,' he said, looking down at the girl.

Megan shot him a warning glance because she knew what was going to come next, but her wishes were ignored.

'I'm your father,' he informed in a voice that held no love at all. It was a matter-of-fact statement and Megan could have cheerfully strangled him. He hadn't changed one iota.

Charlotte hung on to Megan's dressing gown, looking up at him shyly with an expression of awe and reverence on her face. 'Did Santa send you?' she asked in a tiny, breathless voice.

At that he smiled. 'Indeed he did. He told me that there was a very special little girl looking for a daddy.'

Charlotte's eyes were enormous as she turned to her mother. It was clear she thought that some miracle had happened. 'Mummy, isn't Santa wonderful?'

Megan forced herself to smile. 'He always does his best, sweetheart, but it's not Christmas yet, you know.' What else could she say? How could she burst her daughter's precious bubble of happiness? And how the hell had Luigi known?

'It's near enough,' said Luigi. 'How would you and your mummy like to come and spend Christmas with me? I have a great big house and you can help dress the Christmas tree and goodness knows how many presents you'll find under it on Christmas Day.'

'Luigi!' Megan whispered through her teeth. This was emotional blackmail at its worst. Yes, he probably would ply Charlotte with presents, but what the little girl wanted more than anything in the world was a father who loved her, a father who showed his affection in every way possible. Buying a child's love was inexcusable. And that was all he would do, all he would ever do.

And Charlotte was completely overwhelmed, hiding behind her mother's skirts, very warily peeping at Luigi.

'How dare you think you can walk in here after all these years and try to take over my life?' said Megan coldly. 'I have plans for Christmas; why should I change them because of a whim on your part?'

'I can assure you it's no whim,' he told her brusquely. 'I want both you and my daughter back where you belong. I'm giving you no choice.'

Luigi was angry, fiercely angry. His stomach was a tight, knotted ball and he wanted to lash out. He had felt bad enough when Megan left him, but for her to be carrying his child when she did so went beyond the pale. Had she hated him that much? Did she still hate him?

In truth, he hadn't realised that anything had gone wrong with their marriage. Night after sleepless night he'd racked his brains for a possible reason and come up with nothing. He'd thought she was happy, she had no reason not to be. He was a good provider; she'd never been left wanting. He'd worked long hours, yes, but she understood that. It was the only way to get anywhere.

None of her friends or even her parents had known where she'd gone, and his search had proved fruitless. Not even the police could help him. He had immersed himself more deeply into his work, hoping that one day she would get in touch. Finally, though, he'd had to accept that their marriage was over. And he'd worked even harder.

When he'd seen her in his London store he'd been stunned, and when he had looked closely at the little girl he'd known at once that it was his child. He had an old photograph somewhere of his mother at the same age and there was a distinct likeness.

Megan had denied him his daughter and now she was trying to say that he had no rights to her. Lord, she really must hate him. What the hell had he done to her? Of one thing he was sure; he wasn't going to let her get away with it. She was not going to walk out on him again.

'I have no choice?' she questioned now. 'Believe me, no one, and that includes you, makes me do anything I don't want to do.'

He admired the way she stood up for herself. Her bright eyes and prickly stance reminded him of an animal defending its young. And that was exactly what she was doing. But Charlotte was as much his as Megan's.

'Give me a reason why you don't want to spend Christmas with me.' He was sure she had none, except that she no longer loved him. But that was no excuse for depriving her daughter, *his* daughter. He'd never very much liked children, and he'd always worked over Christmas, but all of a sudden he found himself looking forward to taking a few days off and getting to know this beautiful little girl who kept peeping at him from behind her mother's dressing gown.

He would shower her with presents, she would want for nothing, and it would be a Christmas filled with all the good things in life.

And after that? asked his conscience.

After that he would keep her with him, of course. It was her rightful place. Both Charlotte and Megan. He would accept nothing less.

'The reason,' she told him swiftly, 'is that Charlotte doesn't know you. And, to be quite honest, I don't want her to get to know you. An absentee father is worse than not having one at all.'

'What do you mean, absentee father?' he asked sharply. 'You were the one who walked out.'

'Because I never saw you, dammit. What sort of a life was that? And I don't want Charlotte suffering the same way.'

'You belong with me,' he growled fiercely. 'Are you forgetting your wedding vows?'

'Mummy, what's the matter?' Charlotte tugged at Megan's dressing gown, forcing her to soften her face and look down at her worried daughter.

'Nothing, sweetheart. I'm just not sure that I want to go and spend Christmas with your—father.' It pained her to say the word.

'I'd like to go,' whispered her daughter, giving him a timid smile.

Luigi felt exultation. The battle was half won. All he needed now was Megan's acceptance.

'It looks as though you're getting your wish,' she finally managed to choke out. 'You've always been the same, haven't you, Luigi? Nothing ever stands in your way. How many million have you made?'

The question surprised him. 'Enough to buy the whole Gerards Group,' he admitted proudly.

'What?' she asked, her eyes narrowing, a deep, incredulous frown dragging her fine brows together. 'I knew you had ambition but I never imagined that you'd do this well—so quickly.' Gerards was a department store *par excellence*. 'Where are you living these days?'

'I have an apartment right here in the City where I spend most of the week, but my house is in Sussex.'

'Did you know I lived here?'

She looked appalled at the very thought and his lips

twisted bitterly. 'Not at all. I was checking that everything was running smoothly when I overheard this little girl asking Santa Claus for a daddy. It was such an unusual request that I watched as she ran back to her mother. You can imagine my astonishment when I saw that it was you.'

'And so you put your spies on the job and found out where I lived, is that it?' she demanded, her grey eyes bright now with accusation.

'Wouldn't you have done the same if you'd found out that you had a three-year-old daughter whom you knew nothing about?' he countered harshly. 'I find it hard to believe that you've done this to me.'

Megan shrugged, as if she couldn't care less what he thought.

'I think,' he said, 'you'd better get dressed and start packing.'

'Not on your life,' she retorted. He thought she meant that she wasn't going to come at all until she added, 'There's still a whole week before Christmas. And I have to work for a living. I don't finish until Thursday.'

Beginning to fear that he was losing the battle, Luigi snapped his dark eyes and shot her a condemning glance. 'You won't need to work when you're back with me. Give it up.'

She looked beautifully indignant. 'I beg your pardon?'

'I do not want my wife working, it's as simple as that. And may I ask where you leave Charlotte while you're doing whatever it is you do? I hope she's safe.'

'Of course she's safe,' snapped Megan. 'We have a crèche; I can be with her at a second's notice. And I have to work, otherwise how would I keep myself?'

'You won't need to; you're going to live with me,' he repeated impatiently. 'It's your rightful place.' Now that he'd found out he had a daughter he most definitely wasn't going to allow her to escape again.

Megan sucked in a harsh breath. 'You can't tell me what to do. I'm not one of your minions, Luigi; you'd best remember that. Charlotte and I will come to you on Friday, not a day before. And as soon as Christmas is over we're back here.'

He decided not to make an issue of it in front of Charlotte, but he wasn't happy with the situation and he intended to tell Megan so at the very first opportunity. 'I'll send a car for you,' he announced stiffly.

Megan's chin jerked. 'There's no need. Give me your address and we'll make our own way.' She held his gaze, her grey eyes, tinged with amethyst, were as cold and belligerent as his.

'Don't be ridiculous,' he snapped. 'My car will be here at ten. Make sure you're ready. And, Megan,' he added warningly, 'don't try to run away again.'

'Mummy, I like my new daddy. I wanted to go with him,' Charlotte said, pouting, when Luigi had gone.

Megan was peering through the window, watching as he climbed into a sleek black Mercedes. 'I know you did, sweetheart, but Mummy has to work, I can't take time off or I'll lose my job.'

'Will he come back again?'

'I don't think so.' In fact she prayed he wouldn't. 'But it won't be long before we go to his house.'

'Where does he live?'

'I don't know.'

'Why don't we live with him? Laura's daddy lives with them, and Katie's.'

Megan turned back into the room and gathered her

daughter into her arms. 'Sometimes, sweetheart, Mummies and Daddies stop loving each other and they live in separate houses because if they didn't they'd always be arguing.'

'Did you used to argue with Daddy?'

'Not really.'

'So why don't you live together? I want you to. I want my daddy with me all the time.'

How could she explain to a three-year-old that her father was a workaholic and couldn't care less about his family? It wouldn't be the heaven Charlotte thought it would be. Fortunately Jenny phoned at that moment wanting to know if Megan was doing some washing and if so would she throw in her white jeans. By the time their conversation was finished Charlotte had thankfully forgotten her question.

But as far as Megan was concerned her whole day was spoilt. Usually Jenny and her boyfriend lounged about the house and she and Charlotte never had any time to themselves. She had been so looking forward to it. And now all she could think about was Luigi and the fact that they were going to spend Christmas with him.

She ought to have been strong; she should have said no, but how could she deny her daughter what she so obviously wanted? It would be purgatory, she was sure of that. And there was no way on this earth that he could persuade her to move in permanently.

The next four days were sheer hell. She finished her Christmas shopping, not even entertaining the idea of buying Luigi a gift. Why should she? She truly and deeply resented the fact that he was forcing them to spend the festive period with him.

It looked as though another move might be in the cards because she most definitely didn't want to live the rest of her life with a man who hadn't an ounce of love in the whole of his body. It wouldn't even be fair on her daughter to be thrust into such a situation.

Jenny and her fiancé were flying to Paris for Christmas, another reason why Megan had been looking forward to Christmas alone with her daughter, and on Christmas Eve morning it was chaos as they all got ready at once. Finally Jenny and Jake left but Megan had only a short period of breathing space before the car arrived.

She was expecting a polite but indifferent driver and was annoyed to discover that Luigi himself had come to pick them up. Charlotte had been looking through the window and she gave a hoot of delight, though when Megan let him into the house she became suddenly shy again.

'Are you ready?' he asked. He was wearing a suit this morning, an immaculate dark grey with a crisp white shirt and a patterned mustard tie. He was the epitome of the successful businessman, gorgeously handsome to boot, and Megan couldn't stave off a brief flash of the old feelings that had once filled her with such excitement. Had he taken time off work to fetch them? Would he be shooting straight back? It would be good if that were the case because then she and Charlotte could explore his house on their own.

She couldn't help being curious as to where he now lived. Had he sold the house in Derbyshire or did he still own that as well? He had always said how much he loved the Peak District with its beautiful countryside and interesting little villages.

'I'm as ready as I'll ever be,' she admitted.

'So you're still not happy about spending Christmas with me?' he asked, his eyes hard and enquiring on hers.

'No, I'm not.'

'Perhaps I should take Charlotte on her own? Leave you here to—'

'Not on your life!'

He gave a faint smile of satisfaction. Not the sort that reached his eyes and made them crinkle at the corners, not the sort that had once made her reach out to him and kiss him soundly. Nothing like that. It was a getting-his-own-way kind of smile.

'Good, then let's go. Are these your things?'

There wasn't much, two small suitcases. One with their clothes and one with the presents she had bought for her daughter, already wrapped and hidden away from her prying eyes. She saw him look at them doubtfully. 'We'll be coming back for the rest of your stuff after Christmas, I take it?'

'We won't be staying,' she answered evenly. 'Didn't I make myself clear?'

'Perfectly, but I thought you might have changed your mind.'

'I never will,' Megan muttered, keeping her tone low for Charlotte's sake. She didn't want her daughter to hear her sniping at her new-found daddy. But Luigi heard the determination in her tone and his mouth compressed grimly.

He picked up the two cases and headed out to the car. They looked ridiculously small in his hands and as he tossed them into the boot Megan wanted to cry out that she had changed her mind. She had the strongest feeling that if she went with Luigi now it would change her life for ever.

CHAPTER TWO

MEGAN gasped when she saw Luigi's house. They'd left the city behind and headed into the Sussex countryside. He had paused at a set of heavy iron security gates to press a remote control and then driven up a winding drive before coming to a halt in front of a mansion that was perched imposingly at the top of a hill. It was a huge grey stone building with massive Ionic columns forming the front portico, and generous wings flanking the main house on either side.

'*This* is where you live?' she asked incredulously. Charlotte was awestruck too, sitting on the edge of her seat and gazing at the building with wide blue eyes.

'Impressed?' he asked, a dark eyebrow rising expectantly.

'It's not what I imagined,' Megan admitted, but if he thought she was impressed enough to want to move back in with him he was wide of the mark. 'And a little bit grand for one man on his own, wouldn't you say? Unless of course you don't live here alone?'

Her thoughts immediately turned to his very beautiful PA. Was Serena still with him? Was she a permanent part of his life now? When she had first started working for Luigi he had almost constantly sung her praises. So much so that Megan had begun to get suspicious, especially when his long working hours went on late into the night. He had denied it, of course, but her fears had never gone away and it had been part of the reason she had left him.

'I'm alone,' he admitted, much to her relief, because if Serena had been here she would have insisted he take her straight back home. 'For the moment,' he added ominously, looking deeply into her troubled eyes.

Megan ignored it and as they approached the house one of the pair of carved oak doors opened and a dark-suited, white-haired man appeared.

'William, meet my wife, Megan,' said Luigi with a smile. 'And Charlotte, my daughter.'

The man inclined his head. 'Megan, Charlotte,' he acknowledged gravely. 'Shall I show them to their rooms, sir?'

'I'll do it,' said Luigi. 'Tell Cook we're here and we'd like tea in the drawing room.'

Megan was dumbstruck. This was a rags to riches tale in one giant leap. She'd always known he had excellent entrepreneurial skills, but for him to be able to buy Gerards, as well as a house like this in such a short space of time was beyond her comprehension. How had he done it?

And she couldn't help wondering what else he had in mind. A top ranking football club? A luxurious yacht? Exotic holiday homes? It seemed as though the world was his oyster these days. Perhaps he even had these things. But she wasn't disgruntled that she'd missed out because she knew that he would have worked all the hours God gave to get where he was, and that wasn't the sort of lifestyle she wanted.

She and Charlotte were content in their little house, there was always a sense of satisfaction when she paid her bills and cooked and cleaned and provided a happy, carefree environment for her daughter. She wouldn't like to live here, not permanently. It wasn't a home; it was a showpiece.

There wasn't a speck of dust anywhere in the enormous entrance hall, or the shallow, wide staircase they were now ascending. Nothing was out of place. Urns of flowers spilled their heady perfume into the air, while marble statues stood in alcoves and paintings by old masters adorned the walls.

They followed Luigi through long corridors, finally coming to a halt at a suite of rooms, which she presumed to be in one of the wings. He pushed the door open and Megan walked into a blue carpeted room with a four-poster bed draped in matching blue and two armchairs near the window upholstered in cream damask. The curtains at the tall windows were in a cream and blue fabric. It was all very elegant but not her style and Megan felt a faint shudder run through her.

Luigi appeared to be waiting for her to say something, but when she didn't he opened an adjoining door, revealing a further bedroom filled with every imaginable toy possible. Charlotte's eyes widened and she ran inside. 'Are these for me?' she asked in wonderment.

'It's your room,' he told her, 'for as long as you want it.'

'How dare you do this to her,' hissed Megan accusingly as soon as Charlotte had disappeared inside. 'It's nothing short of blackmail. I've not changed my mind. When Christmas is over we're out of here.'

Luigi's lips curved upwards in a knowing smile. 'We'll see about that.'

Meaning over his dead body. Well, that was what she'd do, kill him if necessary. Actually she wouldn't do anything so drastic, but there had to be a way to make him change his mind.

'I'm serious, Luigi,' she told him coldly.

'And I'm serious about you moving back in with me. There's nothing to stop you.'

'Except that I don't love you any more.'

His eyes narrowed suspiciously. 'Is there someone else?'

'There could be.' Why should she tell him that there'd been no one since the day she'd walked out on him? He didn't deserve to know anything.

'Tell me, is there?' he demanded angrily, and he took her by the shoulders and almost shook her. 'Because if there is,' he warned, 'I'm taking Charlotte from you. I won't allow another man to bring up my child.'

Megan was shocked by the ferocity of his tone. 'You're in no position to do anything, so take your hands off me. What I do with my private life is no longer any concern of yours. Charlotte is being well looked after and that's all that need concern you.'

He let out a whoosh of angry air. 'Charlotte needs her father, her biological father. If you're not happy with that then get out. But Charlotte stays.'

Megan couldn't believe he was saying this. A flash of red fury filled her eyes and she lashed out with both fists, raining them on his chest, battering him until she ran out of energy. In response he wrapped his strong arms about her and held her close.

Amazingly Megan felt a stirring of her senses. Lord, this was the last thing she wanted. It had to be anger, a turbulent rage flooding every nerve and tissue. It couldn't be anything else. Could it?

She wrenched away and glared furiously. 'You're a swine, Luigi Costanzo. I can't believe I let myself be bullied into coming here.'

'Bullied?' he challenged. 'Ask your daughter if she was

bullied. She's been deprived, that's what. Why else would she ask for a daddy for Christmas? It's appalling what you've done to her, and I intend to make up for the missing years, have no fear about that.'

A cold chill stole through Megan's veins. 'Is that a threat?' she demanded, standing very straight and rigid and glaring at him through stony eyes.

'If you care to take it that way.'

'What exactly are you saying?'

'That even if you don't want to stay I'm keeping Charlotte.'

This was what she had feared, and the very thought filled her with a dread so deep that the air around her thickened until she found it difficult to breathe. She dragged in huge painful gulps of air. He was serious, and he had the clout to do it. And, unfortunately, it left her with no alternative but to move in with him herself.

But she wouldn't let him know yet that he had her over a barrel. She would fight him every inch of the way. Once Christmas was over, when he'd discovered how much of his time a young child demanded, he might change his mind. Megan felt sure that he had no real comprehension of what it was like to bring up a young, extremely active daughter.

'Bold words, Luigi.'

'I mean them.'

'And have you perhaps thought about Charlotte? She might not want to stay here. It's not exactly what I'd call a homely place.'

He frowned. 'You don't like it?'

Megan shrugged. 'It's imposing, I'll admit that. But it's a statement. It says, look at my lifestyle, look how wealthy I am. It doesn't say that you're happy or comfortable.'

'I don't have time to be comfortable.'

'Precisely. And that is what your daughter would require. Time. *Your* time! How would you give her that when you're busy making your millions?'

'It could be arranged.'

'Arranged,' sneered Megan. 'You make it sound like a business proposition. It wouldn't work, Luigi, and you know it. When Charlotte said she wanted a daddy she meant a full-time one, not someone who would try to fit her in when he could.'

Dark eyes flashed hotly in her direction but he was prevented from saying anything else by Charlotte running back into the room. 'Mummy, come and look what I've got.'

It was sheer madness on Luigi's part, decided Megan, as she studied the mounds of toys stacked in Charlotte's room. Did he think that going over the top like this would make up for the missing years? He really had no idea what a child needed. And the more she thought about his intention to claim Charlotte the angrier she became.

'Didn't you say something about tea?' she asked him sharply, wanting to get out of this room and the obscene number of gifts he had loaded on his daughter.

'Wouldn't you like to unpack first? Or shall I ask—'

'I'll do it,' she snapped, wondering whom he was going to suggest do the job for her. It sounded as though he had a whole army of servants at his beck and call. Was he really happy with this kind of lifestyle?

She backed out of the room and snapped open the locks on her case. It took less than two minutes to hang up their few clothes. The other suitcase with the presents in she left safely fastened. And when she presented herself in Charlotte's bedroom again he was still standing where she had left him. A real father would have got down on his knees and played with his daughter, but not Luigi. He was content to watch; he didn't know how to play. Lord, it made her so mad that he'd cocooned himself in a world where money was the prime factor.

They made their way back downstairs to the drawing room. Again it was carpeted in blue, with display cabinets filled with fine pieces of porcelain. There were two very uncomfortable looking, square-armed chairs and a matching sofa, and on a rosewood tea table in front of them was the tea he had ordered.

The china was delicate, the pot covered by a cosy, and tiny biscuits were arranged on a plate. Hardly the sort of refreshment one would offer a three-year-old, thought Megan, but there were three cups and three small plates, so it looked as though she was expected to join them.

Charlotte ate most of the biscuits but she refused the tea. 'Can I have Coke?' she asked politely.

Megan felt quite amused when Luigi was forced to confess that he didn't have any and Charlotte settled for milk instead.

'We could go shopping,' said Charlotte innocently. 'Me and Mummy always go when we run out of anything.'

'I have to go back to work in a minute,' confessed her father.

Typical, thought Megan. Nothing had changed. But actually it was a relief when he'd gone and she and Charlotte could explore the house together. Her daughter ran from room to room, visibly impressed by the size of the place, but it made Megan angry. Was this what success meant to him? Was he trying to buy happiness? If so he was failing dismally.

As far as she was concerned it was a loveless place and he must rattle round in it. It wasn't a home and she couldn't imagine Charlotte being happy here either. And what annoyed her even more, there wasn't a single Christmas decoration in sight. Why the hell had he invited them for Christmas if he wasn't going to celebrate it?

Megan didn't expect Luigi home for several hours and was surprised when he turned up in the middle of the afternoon with a huge Christmas tree tied on top of his car. Charlotte whooped with delight and all three of them spent the next couple of hours adorning it with the garlands and baubles and strings of flashing lights that he had also brought home.

It reminded Megan of the first Christmas they'd spent together as a married couple. She'd been deliriously happy. They had a home of their own by then and Luigi had walked in on Christmas Eve with a tree, much as he had now. It had taken a long time to dress it because each time she stretched up to hang a bauble he had slid his arms around her and kissed her.

They had called it their loving tree, but as each consecutive Christmas came he worked harder and harder, often not coming home until late on Christmas Eve, and by then Megan had dressed their tree herself. And slowly the magic had gone out of it.

'Look, Mummy, look.' Charlotte was high on her father's shoulders and had just placed the fairy on top of the tree. 'Isn't it beautiful?'

'It's lovely, sweetheart.'

'When's Santa coming?'

'Tonight, when you're in bed.'

'Can I go to bed now?' she asked excitedly.

'No, darling, it's too early.'

'Will he bring my presents here?'

'Of course he will.'

'How will he know I'm here, though?'

'Because he's magic. He knows where all little girls and boys are,' she answered.

Luigi lifted his daughter down and as he did so his eyes met Megan's, and whether it was the magic of the occasion or because she'd been thinking about their first Christmas together, Megan wasn't sure, but she felt a volt of electricity arc through her. She turned swiftly away. It was a warning to be careful. She didn't want to get involved with Luigi again, not at any price. Not unless he changed his lifestyle, and she couldn't see that happening in a hundred years.

It made her increasingly aware how dangerous it had been to come here. She ought to have stood her ground even if it had meant disappointing her daughter. Not that Luigi would have let her. He'd been fully determined to have his daughter for Christmas, with or without her mother.

In fact it might have been safer to let Charlotte come on her own. No! She immediately negated that thought. She would have lost her. Luigi was adamant that he wanted his daughter—permanently. And she was equally as resolute that he would not.

Luigi had felt a warm surge of pleasure as he held his daughter aloft. It was unlike any feeling he'd ever experienced. This was his child, his flesh and blood, something he had created. She was nothing short of a miracle. And he knew that he never wanted to let her go—unlike his handsome Italian father and fun-loving English mother who had never really wanted him, who preferred to go out partying instead of looking after their son.

When he was eight he'd been taken from them and fostered out. Even then he'd been tossed from one family to another because he'd proved to be too much of a handful. He was full of anger and resentment over the treatment he'd received and several times he'd run away, never settling, never knowing what it was like to be truly loved.

It had made him into the tough person he was today. It had made him decide that he was going to make something of his life. He was quick to learn and very intelligent and at sixteen he had left school and started his first job with an IT firm. In fact he'd had a few little money-earners going long before then.

He'd helped school-friends with their homework and charged them. He had good computer skills and published a teenage magazine that was purchased by dozens of his friends both in school and out. He'd bought and sold all sorts of stuff, anything that would make him a profit. By the time he'd left school he'd amassed almost a thousand pounds. But he'd got his eyes set on a million before he was thirty, and he'd succeeded beyond his wildest dreams. He didn't even know what he was worth these days.

Money gave him security, something he'd never had, and he was hurt that Megan didn't like his house. To him it was the pinnacle of all that he'd worked for.

Charlotte was speaking now. 'Do you think, Mummy, that 'cos I asked Santa for a daddy and he's given me one, he won't leave me anything else?'

'Of course he will, sweetheart,' answered Megan, gathering the child into her arms and giving her a great big hug.

Luigi felt an unbelievable sadness. He'd never experienced a mother's arms around him like that. All he'd ever been to his mother was a nuisance, someone to be fed and clothed and told to keep out of the way, often left in the house for long periods alone.

'I expect he'll leave you lots,' he said to his daughter now, and was hurt when Megan gave him a damning look. What did she expect, that he wouldn't give his daughter anything? That he'd given her enough with the few things he'd put into her room? They were nothing, just a few toys to make her feel at home. Wait until tomorrow, she would be the happiest girl alive.

And Megan too; he had no intention of leaving her out, even though she was making it very clear that she wasn't pleased to see him. All that would change, he felt certain, when she realised how much better it would be for Charlotte to have a father as well as a mother.

He couldn't even begin to understand why Megan had kept their daughter a secret. If he hadn't spotted her in Gerards he might never have known. Charlotte would have grown up and had children, *his* grandchildren, and he would have been none the wiser.

The very thought sent a spurt of anger through him and he knew he had to get to the bottom of it. Was Megan being truthful when she said that she'd left him because of the long hours he worked? Or had there been another man involved? Was there still someone else? The one he had seen coming and going from her house, for instance?

Luigi's lips compressed at the thought that there might be some other man in her life. *And in his daughter's life!* This man could be the reason why Megan had been so adamant about wanting to spend as little time with him as possible. He needed to speak to her about it, about *him*, and soon.

The opportunity presented itself as soon as Charlotte had been bathed and put to bed. He'd stood and watched, marvelling at the bond between mother and daughter. It was something he wanted, something he'd missed out on, and he vowed that whatever it took, however much he had to bribe or force, Megan and Charlotte would become a part of his life—for ever!

At least they were still married, that should make things

easier. He wondered why Megan had never got around to divorcing him. On his part it was because he'd never met anyone else he wanted to marry—though there'd been plenty of girls who wanted to marry him. But Megan, what was her story? Did she love the man she shared the house with? What sort of a guy was he that he was content to live with a woman who could never be his in the eyes of the law?

'Asleep at last,' said Megan as she left Charlotte's bedroom and discovered Luigi still lurking. 'She's so excited. Sleeping in a strange house and wondering what Santa's going to bring her is a lot for a little girl.'

'And will it be a lot for her mother, sleeping in a strange house? A house she doesn't particularly like?' he asked, unable to keep the bitterness out of his voice. It had disappointed him that she hadn't been as enthralled as he was. He had expected her to be impressed by how well he'd done. In fact he had hoped that it might prove a deciding factor in bringing them back together.

'I don't expect I'll sleep very much,' she admitted.

'Are you excited about Christmas too?'

'Not on your life,' she retorted. 'I wish I was anywhere but here.'

Luigi felt as though she'd kicked him in the stomach, although, he supposed reluctantly, it had been a big step for Megan to take. She had been honest about why she'd run away and he'd virtually forced her here. Not that he regretted it.

They would both grow to love it, he felt sure. All they needed was time. At least Megan did. Charlotte seemed happy enough, though he wasn't sure whether she'd be so content if her mother didn't stay. In fact he knew she wouldn't. Which made it even more imperative that he persuade Megan to move in with him permanently.

He would need to treat her with kid gloves, which might be difficult because he wasn't used to holding back. And he'd need to show her what she and Charlotte would be missing if she went back to their cramped little house. She'd made it very homely but, given the choice between there and here, he couldn't see there was a choice. This house would win hands down. And he would win too; he would make sure of that.

Couldn't Megan see that Charlotte would be far better off? Not only because of the space in the house, but the grounds as well. There was a copse, a tennis court, a swimming pool, a lake. It was a child's dream. There were even stables, though he had no horses yet. But if Charlotte wanted a pony then it would be hers for the asking.

'It's too early for you to judge whether you're going to be happy here,' he said to Megan now. 'When—'

'It's not altogether the house,' she retorted sharply, 'even though I think it's too pretentious. It's you! You're obsessed with money. You've always been the same. You think you can buy happiness. Well, let me tell you, Mr Rich Guy, you can be happy living in the tiniest hovel, so long as you're with the right person.'

'And you've found the right person?' He couldn't avoid the hard edge to his voice. He wanted to kill the guy, whoever he was. This was his wife.

'I was talking generally.'

She flashed her grey eyes at him and he thought how beautiful she was, still flushed from bathing Charlotte, her hair in slight disarray. His groin stirred and he wanted to pull her into his arms and kiss her—thoroughly. He wanted to prove to her that their love had never gone away; it had simply got lost. 'But there is someone else? I know because you didn't refute it earlier. In fact I've seen him.'

Megan's head jerked, her eyes widened. 'You have?'

'Come and sit down,' he said. 'We need to talk.' He led her downstairs into a cosy little room with panelled walls and a log fire. Red velvet curtains were drawn against the cold winter day and table lamps cast a warm glow. He saw Megan looking around appreciatively. There were a few pieces of antique furniture that he had chosen himself and actually the room was overcrowded, but he quite liked it that way.

'This is my den,' he told her. 'It's—'

'The smallest room in the house,' she finished for him. 'Proving that you don't need a mansion. Big rooms are too impersonal; you can't relax. It's like living in a National Trust property that's open to the public.' She perched herself on the edge of an easy chair.

'So you're saying small is cosy?' He had hoped she would flop down and relax. It looked as though he still had a long way to go. He dropped into the chair opposite so that he could study her to his heart's content, and stretched out his long legs.

'Absolutely.'

'That's why you're happy in your own home?'

'Yes.'

'It's not because you can't afford anything bigger?' Lord, she was more beautiful than ever. What a fool he'd been not to continue his search. He would have promised her the earth if she'd come back to him. Instead he had given up and got on with what really interested him. And it was only now that he realised his mistake.

Megan sucked in a disapproving breath. 'There you go again, bringing money into it. I tell you, money doesn't interest me.'

'You're one on your own, Megan, do you know that?

'Because every other woman you've met has been more interested in your bank balance than you?' she asked sharply.

Her words struck home. It was quite true. He'd never appreciated before he had acquired his wealth how mercenary some girls could be. In one way it pleased him that Megan was different; on the other hand he felt irritated because he wanted her to be excited by what he had achieved.

'It would make life a lot easier for you if you moved in here,' he said, trying his hardest to sound gentle. In reality he wanted to shake her. He had no idea that she could be so stubborn. This was a side of her that had never surfaced in the early years of their marriage.

'No, it wouldn't,' she retorted.

He could see by the glint in her eyes that she meant living with him would be abhorrent, and it hurt. 'You'd never need to work again. That must be every woman's dream?'

'I admit it would be nice not to have to leave Charlotte. On the other hand, she enjoys playing with other children. And soon she'll be at school.'

'Will that make any difference?' he asked tersely. 'What if she becomes ill? Can you take time off work? Would your boss understand? Admit it, Megan, you'd be far better off giving up your job and moving in here. Unless, of course, it's the boyfriend! Is he the one holding you back?'

'So you have been spying on me?' Megan spat the words loudly and, without giving him time to answer, added, 'How low is that?'

He hadn't considered it low. He'd wanted to find out where she lived, what sort of a lifestyle she had. He wanted to make sure she didn't move again. Was that wrong? 'I must confess that when I discovered your address I did sometimes keep watch. Not that it was my intention to spy, Megan. I was hoping to catch sight of you so that we could talk. I would have preferred it that way rather than knocking on your door and giving you the surprise of your life.'

'Fright of my life, more like,' she riposted.

'So, tell me about your boyfriend. He's clearly not asked you to marry him, otherwise you'd have sought a divorce. What does he mean to you? How long have you known him? Does he have a good job?'

'I think,' said Megan tightly, 'that it's none of your business.'

'You're my wife. It's every bit my business,' he challenged.

'In name only,' she retorted. 'Our marriage was over a long time ago.'

'Then why haven't you applied for a divorce?' he asked. This surely had to be in his favour.

Megan shrugged. 'I never got round to it.'

'Because you were secretly hoping that one day we'd get back together?' he suggested.

'You know that's not true,' Megan thrust. 'And, while we're on the subject, let me make it quite clear that I shall never come back to you. Never! So we might as well start divorce proceedings as soon as Christmas is over.'

Stunned by Megan's statement, Luigi sat forward in his chair and looked at her in consternation. 'Divorce? Now! When we've found each other again? When we have Charlotte to consider?' Despite the warmth from the blazing logs a chill radiated out from his heart until his whole body felt as though it were packed in ice. This was the last thing he'd expected—or wanted! She couldn't have given him a crueller Christmas gift.

'I'm perfectly serious,' she retorted. 'We're not compatible, you and I. We each want different things in life.'

'I want Charlotte.' He was adamant on that point. Whether Megan came with her was her problem, but he wasn't letting the child go. She meant more to him than any amount of money. The thought surprised him because previously the state of his bank balance was the most important thing in his life.

'Charlotte doesn't come without me,' she announced. 'And as I have no—'

'You're not being given a choice,' he warned her testily. 'I've got you here now and you're staying whether you like it or not.'

CHAPTER THREE

'IS THAT a warning?' asked Megan, the air constricting in her throat as it closed tightly over Luigi's words. He sounded deadly serious.

'It's not a warning, it's a fact,' he announced. 'And if you dare to defy me I'll have every court in the country on your back. You've denied me my daughter all these years; you can no longer be allowed to get away with it.'

Panic struck in Megan's heart. Could he do it? Had he the right? Surely the courts would find in her favour? Could she afford to take the risk? Was she stuck in this situation? She felt the colour drain from her face and sank back into the chair. 'I can't believe you'd do this to me.'

'You can't? After what you've done to me?' he countered harshly. 'I think you've got away with too much for too long.'

'What if Charlotte doesn't want to stay here? What if Charlotte doesn't like you after she's seen what a bad father you'll be to her? Don't forget I know how much time you spend away from home. She won't like it, she won't be very forgiving.'

'Then I'll have to spend more time here, won't I?' Dark brown eyes seared steadily into hers. He had beautiful eyes; she had always thought that. The whites were very clear and if you looked closely there was a black line around the brown iris. It gave them extra definition, and as he looked at her now she felt that he was seeing right into her mind.

And he was seeing the doubt, the unhappiness, the fear. And he was waiting for her to speak. 'You know you won't,' she flared. 'Maybe for a while, but you'd soon fall back into your old ways. It's a way of life. You wouldn't know what it was like to spend every evening and weekend with your wife and child. You'd be itching to get back to work, to check that things were running smoothly in your absence. You don't know how to delegate. As a matter of fact you don't even know how to play with Charlotte.'

Her rebuke hit home. A dark red flush swept across his face and the air suddenly went chill. 'If I'd been given a chance then maybe I would,' he shot back. 'You're the one who's being unfair here, not me.'

'I like that,' she tossed fiercely. 'You've more or less said that you're going to hold us prisoner—yet I'm the one who's being unfair? I don't think so.'

Luigi jumped to his feet. 'I'm sure that by the time Christmas is over you'll have had the chance to see for yourself that it makes sense. It's time for us to eat. Come, we mustn't keep Cook waiting.'

'I'm not hungry,' protested Megan.

'You will be when you see what culinary delights Edwina has managed to conjure up. She's a marvel in the kitchen.'

Megan reluctantly allowed herself to follow him into the smallest of the two dining rooms where a walnut table had been set for the two of them. It looked very festive with a holly table decoration and red napkins tucked into gold rings, but Megan guessed that there would have been none of these seasonal trimmings if he were eating alone. He probably wouldn't even have been home yet. He would dine out, or make do with a sandwich at around midnight. That used to be his normal practice.

William, the butler, served their meal and Megan found with surprise that she was hungry, very much so.

They started with mango and lobster on a green salad, a combination Megan had never had before, and she found it truly delicious and complementary. 'Is your cook always this inventive?' she asked between mouthfuls.

'Always,' he agreed. 'She keeps urging me to have dinner parties so that she can show off her prowess.'

'And do you?' Megan dabbed a drop of French dressing from her lip with her napkin, an action Luigi watched closely. His eyes on her mouth reminded her of the time on their honeymoon when they'd shared a bowl of strawberries. He had dipped each one in cream and then held it between his teeth for her to take half. And any cream that was left on her lips he had licked off. It had been a truly sexually exciting experience and she dashed the memory away quickly. It was dangerous allowing such thoughts. Besides, such sensual activities had stopped once they were home and work consumed his every waking hour.

The whole meal was a gastronomic experience, making Megan wonder what Christmas Day itself would be like. Her own cooking skills were limited to plain cooking. She ensured Charlotte had a well-balanced diet, they had no takeaway meals or fast food and they ate plenty of fruit, but she wasn't into this type of cookery.

'You're enjoying your meal?' Luigi had hardly taken his eyes off Megan all the time they were eating.

'Very much so,' she said. 'You've found a treasure in Edwina.'

'You could eat her food all the time if you—'

'And I'd end up piling on weight. No, thank you. I prefer my own simple cooking.'

'Maybe I should give Edwina her marching orders?'

'Maybe you ought to get the message that we're not staying,' Megan retorted coolly.

Luigi's lips compressed and he said no more, but even when their meal was finished he wasn't ready to let her go. 'Where do you normally put Charlotte's presents?'

'I fill a stocking from Santa which I put by the fireplace, and a couple under the tree from me.'

'Then we'd better start,' he said.

Megan frowned. 'It won't take a minute; it's too soon. What if she wakes and comes down?'

'If she wakes we'll hear the monitor. I thought it a wise precaution in a house of this size. We don't want her getting lost and upset.'

We, thought Megan, as though he was already of the opinion that they were back together as husband and wife. But maybe it was a good idea to put the presents out because then she could go to bed early and escape him for a few hours. She really wasn't looking forward to Christmas Day, which was a shame because it was normally the highlight of their year.

It wasn't that easy to get away from him, though. After they'd placed their presents—and she was pleased to note that there was only one from Luigi for his daughter—he invited her to join him for a nightcap. Megan wasn't really in the mood but Luigi was insistent, and she knew he wouldn't let her go until she'd agreed.

She couldn't help wondering how things would have been if she hadn't run out on him. Would he be where he was today or would he have become a doting father and spent a lot more time at home? She would never know and, surprisingly, she felt a faint pang of regret that she'd never stopped to find out.

'Would you have ever told me?' he asked, his eyes steady on hers now as he sipped his Scotch.

'About Charlotte?' How had he known what she was thinking?

'Of course.'

'I don't know,' she answered honestly. 'Maybe one day, if Charlotte began asking about you. Not simply, Why haven't I got a daddy?'

'Then I can thank my lucky stars that I was in the right place at the right time. I could have waited a long, long time to meet my daughter.' And with a swift change of subject, 'You're more beautiful than ever, do you know that? Motherhood suits you.'

'Flattery will get you nowhere,' Megan assured him tartly.

His lips curved upwards into a gentle smile. 'It's not flattery for the sake of it, it's the truth.'

They were back in his den, sitting in companion armchairs, the lights turned low, the fire flickering in the grate. The whole house was centrally heated, and she'd never thought Luigi the type to like old-fashioned comforts, but even so it was very welcome. Maybe the fire was in honour of Christmas. There was one already laid in the drawing room fireplace where the tree had been set up. Tomorrow she could imagine it roaring up the chimney, adding to the magic of Christmas for Charlotte.

'Would you have gone to all this trouble if we hadn't been here?' asked Megan, preferring to steer the conversation back to safer grounds. 'I mean the Christmas tree and the log fires.'

'Truthfully?'

'Truthfully.'

'No,' he answered. 'What would have been the point?

This is going to be the best Christmas ever for me—and for you too, I hope.'

'I'm merely here to make Charlotte happy.'

'You're making me happy.'

His voice went down an octave, seeming to vibrate through her bones, and Megan turned her head away, concentrating on her drink, taking large sips of the vodka and orange he had mixed for her. A big mistake; it went straight to her head. Much more of this and she wouldn't be in charge of her senses. 'I've never seen you as the slippers in front of the fire sort of guy.'

'So how do you see me?' he asked with a roguish growl, his eyes reflecting the glow of the embers.

Megan felt them warming her—or was it the fire? Or even the drink? Whichever, she was growing hotter by the second. 'As the tough businessman who's feet never hit the ground. What made you buy Gerards? I thought you were in the IT industry.'

'I still am, but I have my finger in lots of pies. I'll tell you about them some day,' he added dismissively, 'but for the moment I want to talk about you. Why didn't you tell me you were unhappy? Why did you walk out without saying a word?'

'Because I knew you'd stop me,' she retorted, her eyes condemning as she looked at him over the rim of her glass. Her almost empty glass, she realised. 'You'd probably have sworn that you'd change, but I knew differently. And I was right, wasn't I?'

'No one will ever know,' he answered sadly. 'It's hard to accept that I've missed the first three years of my daughter's life—it's something I shall never forgive you for,' he finished harshly as he tossed the last of his drink down his throat. 'Ever!'

Megan finished her drink also and put her glass firmly down on the table. 'I don't want to talk about this. It's late, I'm going to bed.'

As she stood, he too got up, and before she could stop him his arms came around her. 'But you're still my wife, the mother of my daughter, and I'd like a goodnight kiss.'

Megan struggled furiously but he refused to let her go. Instead his mouth came down on hers, one hand behind her head effectively cutting off her escape, the other against the small of her back. It was a long, punishing kiss and it sent resentment reeling through every inch of her body.

There was no escape. The kiss deepened, his arms tightened, and all too soon she felt herself beginning to respond. It was like a replay of when she had met him. She could remember the day very clearly. This handsome, dark-haired, Latin-looking young man had stopped to pick up a bag she'd dropped. Ironically, it had been a few weeks before Christmas and her arms had been full of purchases. When she'd looked into his eyes to thank him she'd been so taken with his good looks that she'd dropped another of her parcels.

'I think,' he said, with a smile that turned her legs to jelly, 'that I'd better help you to your car, or the bus, or wherever you're going. Home, in fact. You've got an extraordinary amount of packages.'

'Christmas presents,' she admitted shyly. 'And I'm catching the bus.'

'I think not,' he said with a laugh, 'not unless you want to lose the lot as you're jumping on or off. I'll run you home; my car's just around the corner.'

'But I don't know you. I—'

'I assure you you'll be perfectly safe. My name's Luigi Costanzo, I live in Mickleover, near Derby.' He flashed his business card in front of her and then tucked it into one of her bags. And Megan knew instinctively that she could trust him. He had an open, honest face, and he had almost to pass her house to get to his own. It would be silly to refuse.

But still she hesitated.

'I know how you must feel,' he said. 'A complete stranger and all that. The offer's there if you want it, but I'll still walk you to the bus stop if that's what you'd prefer.'

Megan was eighteen and he was much older than the boys she usually hung around with. Mid twenties, she imagined, maybe even older than that. She was enchanted by him. And she found herself agreeing to let him give her a lift.

His car was smart, black and sleek. Whatever his business he was clearly doing well for himself. And he drove her straight to her door, even helping her with her parcels. Her parents' eyes goggled when they saw her with a strange, handsome man, but they were clearly impressed.

Before he left, Luigi asked whether he could see her again. Megan couldn't refuse. By this time she was completely bowled over. Her insides felt as though they had turned to mush—*as they were doing at this moment!*

His kiss was awakening all she'd ever felt, and Megan resented it, struggling even more furiously to free herself, until in the end he let her go. There was a twisted smile on his lips. 'Something tells me that old emotions were stirred there. You're not as immune to me as you'd have me believe.'

'Wishful thinking,' she retorted, her lovely grey eyes glaring icily.

'Mmm, we'll see.'

Megan felt a tightening in her stomach. She didn't like the way he said that. He was going to try again, she knew, and it was the last thing she wanted. Damn! How could she respond to him after all this time? She didn't want to be involved with him again, not ever. He wasn't good for Charlotte. A workaholic father was good for no child. She needed two full-time parents.

'Goodnight!' she tossed stormily and marched out.

She felt Luigi's eyes on her but he didn't call her back, and she ran up the stairs as quickly as she could. It seemed to take an age to reach her room, but finally she found it, and closing the door quietly behind her, she stood a moment reflecting on her reaction to his kiss.

It had shocked her beyond measure. She'd thought herself over him. For her feelings to rise so quickly after all these years was scary to say the least.

Perhaps, she tried to convince herself, it wasn't desire— she refused to use the word love, that had flown out of the window a long time ago—it was pure animal passion. After all, she hadn't been with any other man since Luigi; it was natural she would feel something if he—or any man for that matter—kissed her. She was a young, passionate woman with all the feelings that went with it.

Slowly now she walked across the room to check on Charlotte. Her daughter was fast asleep, a faint smile on her lips as though she was dreaming of something nice. Christmas, probably. Or her father. Megan grimaced. Hopefully not! She didn't want Charlotte getting too attached to him because she had no intention of staying, despite Luigi's threats.

Threats! Was that what he was doing, threatening her? It didn't sound nice, and basically Luigi was a nice guy. She'd found that out on the day they met. He had been polite and considerate to her parents and they had immediately taken to him, and in the ensuing days a romance had begun that ended in them getting married six months later. In fact her parents had pushed her into it, declaring she would never find anyone else as good.

She had been the envy of all her friends. Nothing had prepared her for the fact that he put work before everything else. At first she'd been proud of how well he was doing. Before he met her he had written a software program that had taken the computer world by storm, and he had become increasingly busy working on further projects. Sometimes she felt that he thought more of his work than he did her. But then he would come home and their lovemaking reached heights unimaginable. He was every woman's dream in bed, making up a hundredfold for all the time they spent apart.

At least that was what she'd thought in the beginning, but as the months and years had rolled by and he'd never showed her any real affection, she had begun to suspect that their acts of love were merely to satisfy his own basic needs, either that or to ease his conscience because he was bedding Serena. The only time he'd ever declared that he loved her was when he asked her to marry him; even then he hadn't sounded comfortable saying it.

She had become increasingly dissatisfied but if she complained about the way he was never at home he would say that he was doing it all for her, making her feel that she was being selfish. It wasn't until she had found herself pregnant that Megan had known she couldn't bring up her child in a household where there was no love or trust.

Bending over her daughter, she smoothed her soft blonde hair back from her face and kissed her. Charlotte stirred but didn't wake. 'Goodnight, my sweet child,' she whispered. 'Happy dreams always.' And that would only happen if they kept well away from Luigi. Megan wanted Charlotte to grow up in an openly loving family. She was always telling her daughter how much she loved her; Luigi would never do that.

Admittedly, Charlotte was excited now, but it wouldn't last. She would soon find out that her father wasn't the sort of parent she expected and wanted. Not in a million years could Megan imagine Luigi picking up his daughter and swinging her around and telling her how much he loved her. It simply wasn't in him.

It could be that she was doing him an injustice, because after all he'd never been shown any love as a child. But she'd shown him love, so why hadn't he returned it? It wasn't hard to let your feelings flood to the surface. At least she didn't find it so. Luigi obviously did. He kept them all tied up in a knot that he didn't know how to undo. He didn't even try. And she had a sneaky feeling that he might try to buy himself into Charlotte's affections.

Her fears proved true when they went downstairs on Christmas morning and she saw a huge pile of presents almost dwarfing the tree. There was every size and shape imaginable and she was furious with Luigi. He stood there waiting for them, looking extremely pleased with himself.

Naturally Charlotte didn't even look at the stocking Megan had so carefully filled, she ran straight across to the tree. 'Are these all for me, Daddy? Has Santa brought me all these?' Her blue eyes were wide with wonder and excitement.

'Your ones from Santa are over here, sweetheart,' said Megan, taking her hand and drawing her across the room. 'He couldn't carry all those in his sleigh, could he?'

'So where did they come from?'

'From me,' said Luigi, a broad smile on his face. 'Some for you and some for your mother.'

Megan frowned her displeasure. What the hell was he trying to prove?

'But I think your mother wants you to open Santa's presents first.'

He had no idea, thought Megan. Every child in the country this morning was opening their gifts from Santa Claus. Didn't he know that? Not because their mothers wanted it; because it was tradition.

Megan dropped down to her knees and watched as Charlotte tore at the wrappings, her tiny hands trembling. 'Oh, look, Mummy, look,' she kept exclaiming.

'What have you got?' asked Luigi, moving to stand beside her, but not getting down to his daughter's level as Megan had done.

'A new dolly, Daddy, and some clothes for her, and—'

But Megan gained the impression that he wasn't really interested. He wanted Charlotte to open the gifts from him; he wanted to see her pleasure and receive her thanks. He wanted to feel good.

And it wasn't long before Charlotte ran across to the tree. And this time Luigi squatted beside her, enjoying the pleasure on her face as she opened her presents. 'Thank you, Daddy,' she said time and time again, hugging him spontaneously, her shyness forgotten for the moment.

He looked uncomfortable at receiving so much affection, thought Megan, and then wondered whether she was being mean. This was Christmas, after all. A time for giving. She oughtn't to criticise.

She was annoyed, though, at the number of presents he'd bought Charlotte. She was a well-adjusted child, aware that there were some things she wanted but couldn't have, so how dare he undermine her values like this?

Then it was her turn. A whole heap of parcels were for her, and when she begrudgingly opened them, trying her hardest to show pleasure when in truth she felt like throwing them back in his face, she couldn't believe how much he'd spent on her. It looked as though he'd bought up the whole ladies' department at Gerards. Jewellery, underwear, handbags, evening dresses, day dresses, night-dresses, and amazingly all in her size. And the whole of the toy department for Charlotte!

'I haven't bought you anything,' she announced, rather more tartly than she should have done.

'That's all right,' he said pleasantly. 'The fact that you're here is good enough for me.' He gave her a meaningful look over Charlotte's head.

Megan was less than impressed and as soon as she could have a private word with him she went in with all guns blazing. 'You had no right buying Charlotte all those things,' she flared. 'Nor me, as a matter of fact. Have you any idea what you're doing to a young, impressionable child? Are you trying to buy her love, for heaven's sake? You do know she'll come to expect this all the time?'

'So?' he enquired, both hands spread wide, palms facing upwards, a big grin on his face.

'It's not good for her.'

'I have a lot to make up.'

'Nonsense. One gift would have done; she'd have been happy.'

'But I can afford it.'

'I don't care. It's wrong, Luigi. Very wrong! And, let me tell you this, when we leave here she's not taking everything. You've gone over the top and I'm angrier than you can possibly imagine.'

'And beautiful with it. Do you know I never saw you really angry when we were living together. I never saw your eyes flash so dramatically, or your skin colour so beautifully.' His voice lowered conspiratorially. 'It makes me want to take you to bed.'

'Something that is never likely to happen,' she spat.

'Wouldn't you like a little sister or brother for Charlotte?' he asked gruffly.

'Not by you,' she charged.

His face flushed a dull, ugly red. 'And not by that swine you're living with either. Tell him to keep his hands off. You belong to me.'

'Since you never came looking for me I don't see how you can make that claim,' she retorted. 'It proves you weren't interested. I'm even more sure now that it's time to start divorce proceedings.'

CHAPTER FOUR

'NOT on your life,' rasped Luigi. She hadn't a cat in hell's chance of him giving her a divorce.

Megan flashed her magnificent eyes. 'You're nothing more than a materialistic, selfish, uncaring brute. You haven't a loving bone in your body and I want rid of you.'

'Well, think again, sweet wife of mine,' he answered grimly. 'Neither of us is going anywhere. Your place is with me.'

'And wasn't your place with me for the three years I spent with you?' she tossed back scornfully.

For goodness' sake! Why couldn't Megan understand that he had done it solely for her benefit? And he wanted her back—*now*. He wanted Charlotte because she was his daughter, but he wanted his wife because he needed her in bed beside him each night.

How he had missed making love to her. No one else had managed to arouse him as deeply as Megan. Right from the day he'd met her he had desired her, in fact they had constantly devoured each other with their passion. He'd been destroyed when she walked out.

Never for one moment had he thought that it was because of the hours he spent working. He'd provided for her every need, she'd wanted for nothing, and they'd made love with amazing frequency no matter how tired he felt, so had that really been the reason? Or was she making excuses?

Had she fallen for someone else? That guy she was now living with, for instance. Only one thing pleased him about that relationship; Charlotte didn't call him Daddy. Otherwise she wouldn't have wished for a daddy for Christmas.

And what did her boyfriend think about Megan coming here for the holiday period? Was he angry or understanding? He had to be the reason Megan wanted to keep her visit as short as possible. Maybe he ought to talk to him. Tell him he was wasting his time, that Megan belonged to him and he was taking her back.

'Things are different,' he told her now, trying to keep his voice low. 'I don't need to work so hard. I have people who do it for me. Believe me, Megan, you can come up with all the excuses in the world but none of them hold any water.'

'How do I know you're not saying this simply to get me to change my mind?' she demanded fiercely.

Lord, how beautiful she looked on this Christmas morning in her button-through red dress, which fitted her narrow waist and flared elegantly over her hips and thighs. She had gorgeous legs, long and slender, and he couldn't help remembering the times she had wrapped them around him as they made love. He could even imagine the feel of her against him now and he made a half move towards her, his heart hammering against his ribcage.

But the glare in her lovely eyes stopped him. 'We shouldn't be having this conversation,' he said. 'I want this day to be as perfect for you and Charlotte as possible.'

'Some hope of that,' she hissed beneath her breath but he ignored it and turned to his daughter instead, who was skipping from one present to another, unsure of which to play with first. It filled his heart with joy and pride to watch her, and he knew in that moment that he was never going to let her go. He would fight Megan tooth and nail if necessary.

All of a sudden Megan glanced through the window. 'Charlotte, look,' she said urgently, 'it's snowing.'

They all three went to watch as big white flakes settled on the lawn and then melted again just as quickly.

'Can we go outside?' asked Charlotte excitedly.

'Of course, sweetheart,' answered Megan, thankful for the distraction. But Luigi came too and he and Charlotte tried to catch the falling flakes. He was a little awkward at first, playing with her, but after a while he began to relax and ran around the garden while she chased him.

But all too soon the snow stopped, there was not even enough to cover the ground, and they all trooped back indoors. By this time they were thoroughly late for breakfast and Cook tutted as she served their meal. 'I bet it's ruined,' she complained.

'It's not your fault, Edwina,' said Luigi, trying to placate her. 'We didn't want to miss the snow, did we, Charlotte?'

Charlotte, suddenly shy again, shook her head, staring with wide blue eyes at the plump motherly woman who was standing arms akimbo watching to see whether their bacon and eggs were edible.

Megan took a mouthful and smiled. 'It's perfect. Thank you very much, and I'm sorry we held you up.'

The woman suddenly beamed. 'That's all right, lass, it is Christmas after all.'

The whole day passed in a whirl of talking and eating and playing and Megan began to feel that it might not be so bad after all living with Luigi. He was undoubtedly making an effort. The question was, would it last?

It was not until Charlotte was in bed that Megan and Luigi were finally alone.

'Have you enjoyed your day?' she asked as she curled up on a chair in Luigi's den. 'Has Charlotte worn you out? Did you find it easy coping?'

'If you're asking whether I've changed my mind the answer's no,' he retorted sharply, his eyes narrowed on her face. 'I'm even more determined now. This is the ideal place for a child. She's had the time of her life, surely even you can see that?'

'She enjoys herself every day,' flashed Megan, not having expected such a sharp rejoinder. 'A palace or a cottage, it makes no difference. What wouldn't be good for Charlotte is you spoiling her. You've bought her far too many toys, and as for the computer, how old do you think she is, for goodness' sake?'

Luigi shrugged. 'I simply instructed my toy department to pack up whatever they thought suitable for a nearly four-year-old.'

'You did what?' exclaimed Megan disgustedly. 'You didn't even choose one thing yourself? How appalling is that? Did you issue the same instructions for my presents? Damn you, Luigi! You can take the whole lot back after the holiday. I don't need them and I don't want them.'

A muscle jerked in his jaw, telling her that she had hit a raw nerve, but she didn't care; it was true. What sort of a cop out was that?

'Don't be ridiculous,' he snorted. 'You're overreacting. How the hell am I supposed to know what a young child likes?'

'You could have made it your business to find out. Or would that have been too much trouble?' she demanded coldly. 'It seems to me that you've grown too big for your boots. It's easier to pay someone else to do your chores. I don't think I want to hear any more of this. I'm going to my room. I should have known that Christmas would turn out to be a disaster.'

But she hadn't even reached the door before Luigi was on his feet barring her exit. And when she tried to push her way past him he enclosed her in his strong arms. 'I refuse to spend the evening alone,' he told her tersely. 'You're not walking out on me.' And before she could even begin to struggle, before she could even guess his intentions, his mouth possessed hers.

It was Megan's undoing. It sent a whole storm of sensations spiralling through her and although she knew that she ought to push him away she did nothing, she actually revelled in the feelings he created. He always had been a fantastic lover and it took her no more than a few seconds to realise what she'd been missing. Lord, if this kept up she would be begging him to make love to her. What sort of a Christmas present would that be?

And, excitingly, it did keep up. She hadn't the will-power to stop him. Every vein and artery went on to red alert, responding and leaping out of control. She kept telling herself to fight him, to put an end to this joy, but how could she? Her body was starved. She hadn't realised it until this moment but it was now telling her that it wasn't natural to go so long without the attention of a man.

That the man should prove to be Luigi was ironic to say the least, but better the devil you know came the immediate thought, and Megan returned his kiss, parting her lips to allow him entry, moving her body against his, feeling the source of his own passion. He groaned deep within his throat and took advantage of the fact that she wasn't rejecting him.

Just this one kiss, decided Megan, then she would carry

on up to her room. Easier said than done. That one kiss lasted for an infinite period of time. That one kiss turned into a full-scale sex alert.

'You're still the sexiest woman in the universe,' Luigi said in a hoarse passion-filled voice. 'I must have been crazy to let you go.'

Not half as crazy as she felt at this moment, decided Megan, her hands on the back of Luigi's head, her fingertips digging in, unconsciously revealing the fact that she didn't want this moment to stop.

Luigi's hands slid down to her bottom and pulled her firmly against him, his deep groans revealing the desire that raged in his tautly honed body. When she didn't object he swung her up into his arms and carried her over to the soft leather sofa.

Megan lay there and looked at him, her breathing unsteady, her grey eyes luminous and filled with a sexual hunger that she hadn't felt in years. Ought she to put a stop to it, or let nature and their animal hunger take its course? Would she live to regret it, or would she view this occasion as a fitting end to their tragic marriage? Maybe she could even use it as a form of revenge? Let Luigi see exactly what he was missing. Allow him this one last chance to make love to her and then leave him high and dry. She smiled at the thought.

'What's funny?' he asked as he sat on the edge of the sofa and stroked a gentle finger over her lips.

'Private thoughts; nothing you'd understand.' Or appreciate, she added silently, nibbling the end of his finger.

He drew in a swift breath. 'How I've missed you,' he murmured, his eyes darkening, his hand sliding possessively over her breast.

It hardened beneath his touch, her nipple leaping into

ecstatic response, and Megan closed her eyes, her mind suddenly confused. This was a dangerous game. She ought to get out now while she still had the strength. But already it was too late. Luigi had popped the buttons on her dress and with a speed perhaps born of desperation he sucked first one and then the other nipple into his mouth right through the thin fabric of her bra.

Megan was lost. She had always loved him doing this to her. It created the most exquisite feelings, making her arch towards him, giving freely, wanting everything that he had to offer.

The sane part of her mind told her that she was making a mistake when he moved her from the sofa to the softly carpeted floor, when he stripped off his clothes with indecent haste and then began to undress her somewhat more leisurely. At least that was his intention but Megan couldn't wait. She tore off her dress, swiftly followed by her undies, and they fell on each other with a hunger created by the years they'd spent apart.

Luigi had always been a brilliant lover, she couldn't deny that, and nothing had changed. Although he was desperate he was still solicitous of her needs, making sure that she had no last minute regrets.

How could she when her body raged with desire so deep that it almost hurt? Their bodies moved together in a rhythm as ancient as time and he allowed her to reach her climax first, to revel in wave after wave of exquisite sensation, before he too gave up the fight and wrestled with his own delirious torture.

As the convulsive movements of his body slowed and finally came to a stop he turned to her with a smile. 'Just like old times, eh?'

Megan nodded. How could she deny it? Nevertheless it

wasn't going to happen again. She had succumbed to her bodily needs without consulting her head. A major mistake. Not that she regretted it; how could she regret such feverish passion? She had missed this part of their relationship without even realising it. Her body had become almost barren and now it was alive again.

'Do you still want to go up to your room?'

'No,' she whispered, her throat aching with the pleasure she'd just experienced.

And as they lay there in each other's arms Luigi reached for her again. This time there was no urgency; they were able to take their time rekindling all the delicious excitement that had once been theirs.

When Megan finally lay in her bed she felt as if she were floating on air. Her body had been taken over by forces beyond her control. There was no thought in her mind about escaping back to her own home; her place was here with Luigi.

Luigi, who was in bed beside her!

He'd wanted her to join him in his own bed but Megan had refused. 'What if Charlotte wakes and can't find me? She'll panic.'

'Then,' he'd announced in a deep, sexy growl, 'I'll share yours.' And there had been no hope of saying no to him.

He lay on one elbow now looking at her, a gentle finger exploring the contours of her breasts, his eyes, so dark with pleasure, stirring fresh emotions. Where they all came from Megan had no idea. She couldn't quench her thirst for him. Nor could he, for that matter.

'We have a lot of time to make up,' he murmured, honing in on her thoughts.

Megan smiled, her eyes softening and warming. 'And you propose doing it all at once?'

'I intend to try.'

'How do you suggest we cope with a spirited child tomorrow if we have no sleep?'

'Uh oh!' He slapped a hand to his head. 'I'd forgotten. I'd imagined spending the whole of Boxing Day in bed. Edwina bringing us up our meals while we did our best to catch up on the missing years.'

'Think you could manage?' she taunted, her eyes alight with wicked pleasure. She had never in her wildest dreams imagined that this was how the holiday would turn out. And the most amazing thing was that she didn't mind. She was actually enjoying it. She had shut out of her mind the fact that all too soon Luigi would be back at work and this honeymoon period, if she could call it that, would be over. She was taking every minute as it came and making the most of it. It was the wrong time of the month for her to conceive, so she wasn't even worrying about that.

Luigi couldn't believe his good fortune. He hadn't even had to work on Megan; she had fallen into his arms as naturally as if they had never parted. Elation filled his very soul and there was no doubt in his mind that she would now move in with him and they would become a proper family.

It would change his life. He was a father! He wanted to shout it from the rooftops. And what a gorgeous little girl she was. Megan had done a brilliant job bringing her up so far, and now he would be here to help. Long hours would be a thing of the past. Charlotte needed him. And he needed Megan!

Hungrily he reached for her again but she had fallen asleep. He smiled and with his arm across her body he too drifted into the world of the unconscious.

They were woken by Charlotte's highly excited voice.

'Mummy, wake up! It's snowing again. Daddy, it's snowing. Come and look.'

As they were both naked under the bedcovers they waited until Charlotte had turned to the window before Megan dived for her dressing gown and Luigi whipped a sheet off the bed and tucked it around his loins in double-quick time.

They were laughing as they joined Charlotte and it pleased him that his daughter had made no comment about finding them in bed together. It meant that she'd accepted him unreservedly as her father, and as Megan had welcomed him with open arms too the future looked good.

The snow fell more heavily than the day before and began to stick to the ground. It was so rare to have a white Christmas, thought Megan, that it had to be a good omen. In fact she was glad that she'd let Luigi persuade her to join him.

Later in the day they snowballed each other and made a snowman and Luigi let his hair down more than Megan had ever seen before—except in bed, of course. There were no inhibitions there. He was, if anything, a better lover.

There was the faint niggling doubt in her mind that he had gained extra experience with other girls, but she swept it away—it was her fault if he had—and if he had enhanced his sexual prowess then she ought to be grateful. The many different ways he'd pleasured her had been utterly fantastic. She only had to think about it to experience a resurgence of the feelings that had danced excitedly inside her.

Her eyes sparkled whenever she looked at him and Luigi gave her slow, intimate smiles that told her he knew exactly what she was thinking. 'Later,' he mouthed and Megan hugged the precious thought to her. She couldn't wait. It was like a replay of when they first met and couldn't get enough of each other.

Before he had become a tycoon and work was more important!

She dismissed the thought as immediately as it entered
her head. Luigi was a father now, he had a different set of
responsibilities. He wouldn't let Charlotte down.

Neither of them could wait for their daughter's bedtime.
Luigi followed Megan to the bathroom and watched her
bathing Charlotte. What an amazing mother she was, so
gentle, with a glow about her that touched his heart. But
his fingers curled into his palms when he recalled how she
had cheated him out of seeing his daughter born, of sharing
the first few precious years of her life, even preparing for
the birth. Not that he was going to let that spoil his pleasure
this evening.

He'd been looking forward all day to making love to
Megan. She had matched him step for step last night and
judging by the way she kept looking at him, her beautiful
eyes full of passion and desire, she was quite willing to
allow him into her bed again.

And he was not disappointed. From the very moment he
slid his arms around her the years they had spent apart dis-
solved into the mists of time. She was his again, completely,
urging herself against him, her hunger as deep as his own.

She kissed him with the sensuality that only a woman
deeply in love could give. And it amused him to let her take
the lead—for now! She touched and kissed and stroked,
enjoying the fact that she could arouse him by a simple
kiss, or the lightest touch of her fingertips, her actions
becoming more and more urgent until in the end he could
contain himself no longer.

'No more,' he growled, laying her on her back and positioning himself over her. Then he took her, instantly and fiercely, and her cries of pleasure matched his as the intense joy of making love filled their hearts and minds. It was a long time before their sweat-slicked bodies stopped writhing in the aftermath of exquisite pleasure, before their breathing returned to normal.

'That was quite something,' he muttered hoarsely. 'Lord, am I glad I found you again.'

Megan didn't answer. She had her eyes closed and a blissful expression on her face. In fact he had never seen her look more beautiful. Every feature was softened, and her skin had a lustrous glow. She looked like a woman who was extremely satisfied. He was sure now that she wouldn't walk away from him again.

They made love twice more before falling asleep in each other's arms. And for the first time in his life Luigi didn't feel the urge to be up at dawn and at his desk. He had a woman at his side whom he had almost lost; he wasn't going to risk it again. He would go, eventually, and he would work sensible hours, but for the moment Megan was more important.

Except that it didn't work out like that.

Halfway through the morning he and Charlotte were snowballing each other once again, when Megan, who had gone indoors for a handkerchief for her daughter, marched out of the house with her face as black as a thundercloud and slammed the phone into his hand. 'A call for you.'

He frowned. 'Who is it?'

'Find out for yourself,' she snapped, and taking Charlotte's hand she dragged her protestingly into the house. He faintly heard her say, 'Come on, let's get packed, we're leaving.'

One half of him wanted to chase after her, find out what

was going on, the other needed to know who was on the other end of the phone. Whoever it was had clearly upset his wife.

'Can I speak to Luigi, please?' The woman's husky voice still echoed in Megan's ears.

'May I ask who's calling?'

'Tell him it's Serena,' came the sultry answer. 'And hurry please; I haven't got all day.'

Serena! So she *was* still on the scene! The thought sent her sick to the pit of her stomach. 'How dare you speak to me like that?' retorted Megan. 'I'm not one of his servants.'

'I don't care who you are,' riposted the woman. 'I want Luigi.'

'You want him, do you?' snapped Megan, unable to keep the anger out of her voice. 'Then it's bad luck you're having because he's not available.'

'I think Luigi will be available if you tell him who I am.'

'You think you'd take preference over his wife?' It crucified Megan to think that Luigi had jumped into bed with her while still carrying on an affair with his PA. But she wasn't going to let Serena know that.

'He and his wife are long since parted,' sneered the other woman. 'He's a fool not to have divorced her. How she could walk out on him, I have no idea. He's—'

'Actually she's walked back into his life,' rasped Megan. 'You're speaking to her right now.'

There was a long silence.

'But I'll still get him for you, if that's what you want,' she added, her voice sickly sweet. 'Just one moment.' And she didn't stop to listen to what else the girl had to say. She was sick to the bottom of her heart as she walked out of the house and tossed the phone to him.

His eyes said it all. He was torn two ways. And it told

her what she needed to know. If he truly cared about her, if he truly wanted them to get back together, he would have ignored Serena's call and followed her. Instead she heard him speak softly into the phone, turning away so that she wouldn't hear.

CHAPTER FIVE

'IS SERENA still working for you?' Megan didn't really want to know and yet she couldn't stop herself. She wished she could take the question back because it made her sound jealous, and why should she be? As Luigi was no longer a part of her life she couldn't care less how many women he was involved with.

Liar!

It wouldn't have mattered before she slept with him, but it did now. He had treated her as though she were the only one. No, that wasn't strictly true. He had made her *feel* as though she were the only one. A big difference! It could be that he was an artist at it. How did she know what he was like these days? His main aim at the moment was getting custody of his daughter. And if the mother came as part of the package then he was home and dry. A ready built babysitter while he was free to work his long hours and continue his affair.

Megan was furious by the time she'd worked all this out and had already packed before confronting Luigi. She had seen him out of her bedroom window talking into the phone. She had observed the way he stood, the way he moved his head as he listened, the way he moved his hands—as though he was touching Serena in his mind's eye. It all suggested that he was speaking to a woman who meant a great deal to him. It even looked as though he blew her a kiss when he finished.

'As a matter of fact, yes, she is,' he answered easily. 'But you don't need to worry your pretty head about her.'

'I don't?' Megan retorted, her tone so sharp that it was a wonder it didn't slice into him. 'She made it sound pretty clear to me that she was number one priority in your life.'

'In my business life,' he pointed out. 'Serena's my PA. You know that.'

'Really?' Megan allowed her finely shaped brows to ride smoothly upwards, her grey eyes totally disbelieving. 'Is that *all* she is? It wasn't the impression I got. And if you believe I'm going to move back into your life when she is clearly a part of it then think again. All I can say is thank goodness Serena rang because now I know exactly where I stand.'

'Don't be ridiculous, Megan,' barked Luigi. 'Serena means nothing to me. You and Charlotte mean everything.'

'I wonder if you'd be saying that if I hadn't walked out on you?' she accused. 'I wonder whether fatherhood would have made you change your lifestyle? Somehow I don't think so. You feel cheated, yes, and because Charlotte's lawfully your daughter you want her, but that's as far as it goes.'

'Are you suggesting that the last two nights meant nothing to you?' he demanded, his brow thunderously dark, his whole body taut with suppressed emotions.

'All they've done,' she riposted smartly, 'is remind me of what an expert lover you are. But good sex is all it was. It didn't mean anything.' She'd been love-starved, that was what, and she *had* enjoyed it, but it went no further than that.

His dark eyes flashed. 'I don't believe you.'

'Believe what you like,' she tossed back, 'but I'm out of your life for good. Serena's welcome to you.'

'You'd ruin your daughter's happiness?' he accused. 'Her life as well, by depriving her of the father she's just found? Whom she needs, I might add, as much as she needs her mother.' His eyes were glacial, as hard as the ice that had formed in the cracks in the paving outside.

Megan hadn't looked at it from this angle. Would it be bad for Charlotte? Or would it be better to make a clean break now before her daughter really got to know Luigi? She knew the answer even before she began debating it. Charlotte needed her father. It was that simple. She'd been so happy when she discovered she did have a daddy after all. It would be cruel to deprive her of him now. Except that she didn't want a part-time father for Charlotte. Nor indeed a father who bedded other women!

'I'll stay on two conditions,' she told him stonily, reluctantly.

'And they are?' he demanded.

Who would have thought, Megan asked herself, that a few short hours ago they'd been making love? Where had all the pleasure gone? They were facing each other like two sworn enemies out for the kill. She lifted her chin. 'Number one, that you cut your working hours. And number two, there are no other women in your life.'

'Done,' he said easily and far too quickly for her peace of mind.

'I'm serious,' she countered.

'And so am I. You and Charlotte mean everything to me.'

'And Serena?'

He gave a tiny shake of his head, as if to say, Why do you keep questioning me about Serena? 'She's my right hand,' he told her calmly. 'I can't cut her out of my life, she virtually runs it—on a business level, of course,' he added when he saw the accusing glint in Megan's eyes.

'And was business the reason she rang now?' charged Megan. Because it hadn't seemed like that to her. The woman had sounded sickly possessive.

'Of course! Which reminds me—' he shot back his cuff and looked at his watch '—I'm needed. I have to go. And when I return we'll go to your house and collect the rest of your stuff. You will be here?' he added when he saw the doubt in her eyes.

Megan realised with a pang that she had little choice. Charlotte's future security and happiness depended on it.

As Luigi drove to his office he felt faintly uneasy. He wasn't completely sure that Megan would still be there when he got back. On the other hand, the fact that she'd sounded jealous of Serena had to be a good thing. If she *was* jealous then it could mean that she still had feelings for him. It could be to his advantage, except that he would have to tread a fine line. He couldn't afford to let Serena upset Megan.

Serena was excellent at her job, he didn't know what he'd do without her, and he sometimes rewarded her by taking her to dinner or the theatre. That Serena fancied herself in love with him he was fully aware, but the feelings weren't mutual. Even though he had lost all hope of Megan returning he'd never wanted anyone to take her place. He kept his lady friends at a distance and usually they got the message—except for Serena. He wondered exactly what she had said to Megan. Perhaps he should ask her?

But the opportunity didn't present itself. He ran his whole empire from a top floor suite of prestigious offices in London's regenerated dockland area, where the views on a clear day were far reaching. Today he didn't have time to look out of the windows. A problem had occurred at one of his IT companies where a disgruntled employee had fed a virus into a software programme that had been released for Christmas. It had already begun to reveal itself and he needed to recall all copies before any real damage was done.

It was after eight by the time he arrived home. He had phoned Megan from his car on the way, half-expecting her to be gone, relieved when she wasn't, and not surprised that she sounded angry.

He found her curled up in a chair in the sitting room, so deeply engrossed in a book that she didn't hear him enter. Except that the book was upside down! He smiled faintly and spoke her name and she looked up with a very creditable start.

'So you've finally torn yourself away from Serena,' she accused, her magnificent eyes flashing daggers at him. Their usual grey had become a soft amethyst, reflecting the colour of the purple sweater she wore. He had noticed this before—whichever colour she wore, her eyes seemed to change with it. It fascinated him.

'I did explain on the phone,' he told her patiently. At least he hoped he sounded patient. She didn't make it easy for him. What he would like to do was give her a good shake—except that it would get him nowhere. But patience never had been one of his virtues.

'And was it only this morning that you promised to work less hours?' she continued. 'Such a short memory you have. Why am I surprised?'

'There were extenuating circumstances,' he reminded her sharply. 'Weren't you listening when I—?'

'Oh, yes, I heard everything you said,' Megan cut in with exaggerated calm.

'But you don't believe me? Well, you'd better because it will be spread all over the newspapers tomorrow. We've already had several reporters sniffing around. This could ruin the company.'

'And do you know who did it?'

'Actually, yes. Before leaving he bragged to one of his colleagues that he would bring the company to its knees. It's a pity he wasn't taken seriously. It's going to be one big headache for the next few days, weeks, months maybe.'

'Meaning you'll be working all the hours God gave again?'

'I'll try not to.' But he could see by her expression that she didn't believe him, and he couldn't answer in all honesty that he wouldn't. He was a hands-on type of guy who never believed in passing the buck. 'Let's go and collect your stuff. I'll instruct Amy to keep her eye on Charlotte.'

'At this hour?' she demurred, slowly uncurling her legs and sitting up straight. Amy was the maid, a giggly brunette girl who was always willing to please.

Luigi wondered if Megan had any idea how gorgeous she looked. Her face was bare of make-up and she could have passed for eighteen. His male hormones stirred and he wanted to take her to bed, but he forced sanity to prevail. 'Why not?'

'Of course, you'll be working late again tomorrow,' she scorned. 'It's now or never, isn't it? Maybe it wasn't such a good idea to—'

'You're not changing your mind,' he cut in swiftly and fiercely. No matter what it took, he was determined not to lose Megan again. 'Get your coat; we're leaving now.'

To his relief she did as he asked, running down the stairs a couple of minutes later in a camel-coloured winter coat with a red scarf tossed casually around her neck. It would be warm in his car but it was jolly cold outside, and he guessed her house would be cold too.

'I presume you're going to put your house on the market,' he said, after they'd been driving for a few minutes in silence.

'It's rented,' she corrected him.

'So what's the procedure? Will the landlord accept a lump sum in lieu of notice?'

'I share,' she told him flatly.

Luigi felt his guts tighten. He'd almost forgotten the boyfriend. Oddly, Megan hadn't seemed too concerned about leaving him. It wasn't a nice feeling to realise that he didn't know the way his own wife's mind worked. In fact, had he ever really got to know her? Hadn't he been too immersed in his own business dealings? Physically, they'd both been fulfilled, but mentally and spiritually? A brief sadness filled him. 'What do you think he'll have to say about you moving in with me?'

'He? Oh, Jake. There's not much he can say, is there? I'm still legally married to you.'

She sounded remarkably calm and for some reason it angered him. 'If you think you're still going to see him, then you can forget it,' he barked.

'Have I said I will?'

Could it be that he was blowing the whole thing up out of all proportion? Perhaps this Jake fellow meant nothing to her. Maybe it was a cost-effective arrangement. But he couldn't be sure and the thought of Megan sharing a bed with another man, the thought of her thrashing about with the same uninhibited responses, made his blood run cold.

'No, you haven't and you'd damn well better not,' he warned tersely. 'In fact, if he's there tonight I'll tell him myself. In fact I'll—'

'You don't have to worry,' she cut in. 'He's in Paris— with his fiancée.'

Luigi pulled the car into the side of the road and tugged on the handbrake. 'What did you say?'

'Jake's with Jenny in Paris for Christmas. Jenny's my housemate.'

'So why the hell didn't you tell me that in the beginning?' he roared, hating the idea that she'd made a fool of him.

'I found it amusing that you jumped to the wrong conclusion.'

'Well I don't find it amusing,' he retorted. 'I've suffered all sorts of horrors imaging you in bed with him.'

'There's nothing you could have done about it,' she pointed out. 'But do you really think I'd have agreed to move in with you if I was involved with someone else?'

He had thought he'd given her no choice; now he began to realise that Megan had had the upper hand all the time. 'I like to think that you would, for Charlotte's sake,' he told her grimly. He restarted the engine and drove fast and furious and silent until they reached their destination.

The house was freezing and he hadn't been as sensible as Megan and pulled on an overcoat. 'I hope your pipes haven't frozen,' he said testily, rubbing his hands together. 'You really shouldn't leave it unheated like this, you could have a burst.'

'And who'd pay the fuel bills?' she retorted smartly.

'So how's your friend going to manage?'

Megan shrugged. 'Maybe Jake will move in. What I do know is that she won't be very happy when she discovers that I've left without giving her notice.'

'Don't worry about that,' said Luigi offhandedly. 'I'll see that she's not out of pocket.'

'Here we go again,' she derided as she flung clothes into

the suitcases she had brought back with her. 'Money solves all problems, that's your maxim, isn't it? Well, it's not mine, and I don't want you insulting Jenny by offering her money.'

Luigi was quite sure that her friend wouldn't be insulted. In fact he'd like to stake a bet that she'd be hugely grateful for any handout. What person wouldn't? But he didn't say this to Megan because he knew what sort of a response he would get. Instead he said, 'You know her best.' He fully intended, though, to see that the other girl didn't lose out because he had spirited her housemate away.

'When are your friends coming back?'

'I'm not sure. Tomorrow, I think,' she told him bluntly, reaching down a holdall from the top of her wardrobe and throwing in toiletries and other bits and pieces that he presumed she couldn't live without. Personally, he would rather she left them behind and he bought her a whole load of new stuff. But with the fuss she'd made about the Christmas presents he knew he dared not suggest it. Megan had become a highly independent lady.

Finally she wrote a note for Jenny and placed it on the kitchen table. 'OK, I'm ready,' she said. 'Let's go.'

He would have liked it better if she looked happy about it. Instead a scowl marred her lovely face. It wasn't going to be the happy union he'd hoped for. But given time… And a lot of persuasion on his part! And no working long hours! Though how he was going to achieve that he didn't know. There were always problems of one sort or another to be dealt with. Yes, he had managers, very good ones, but he liked to be kept informed at all levels. It was why he was so successful. Surely Megan could understand that?

'I wish you could be happy about this,' he said as they began their journey home.

Megan sighed and said nothing.

'If I'd known how unhappy you were before I would have done something about it. Why didn't you say?'

'Because it wouldn't have mattered, you'd have still gone your own way,' she retorted sharply. 'I couldn't stand living in an empty world any longer. And I pray I'm not making the same mistake again. I'm not sure that I'm doing the right thing even now, but I'll give it a try for Charlotte's sake.'

That night Megan wouldn't allow Luigi into her bed. Lord, she wanted to, she even ached for him, but the Serena issue prevented her. She didn't tell him it was because of his PA, but he guessed anyway.

'You're making a huge mistake,' he told her grimly, as they stood outside her bedroom door. Charlotte had been bathed earlier and they'd sat in his den with their now ritual night-time drink. 'Serena is not and never has been my bed partner.'

'But she'd like to be? And you've taken her out? There's more to it than a professional relationship?'

Luigi drew in a deeply pained breath. 'She'd like there to be,' he admitted.

'And you're strong enough to withstand the allure of a beautiful woman?'

'Serena, yes.'

Megan's eyes narrowed. 'So there have been others?' Her tone was deeply accusing.

'You can't blame me,' he rasped, his eyes dark and resentful. 'I'm a red-blooded male, full of sex hormones that need feeding now and then.'

'So that's what I was doing, feeding your hormones?' Megan's head began to spin. It was one way of putting it, she supposed. He'd always been highly sexed with a hot-blooded

Latin male possessiveness that had at one time thrilled her, but now sent a sickening chill into the very heart of her soul. She fed his need; it was as simple as that. And she had compromised herself by agreeing to move in with him!

He had a lot to prove before she'd allow him into her bed again—and if he dared to let any other woman assuage his sexual urges then she'd be out of here quicker than he could say I'm sorry.

'You're different, Megan, you should know that. You're my wife, you're mine, and we need each other. Haven't we proved it?'

He stood close and she could smell the very maleness of him. It excited her beyond measure but she knew that she had to be strong. 'I need you like I'd need a boil on the end of my nose,' she spat. 'I've managed very well, thank you, for the last four years. The only reason I've agreed to stay is for Charlotte's benefit. But if you give me hell, like you're doing at this moment, then I'll run away again.'

'You'd be that selfish?' he blazed. 'You'd deprive my daughter of her father's guidance just because *you*—' he stabbed the word incisively '—can't handle the idea that while we've been parted I've had other girlfriends. God dammit, woman, I didn't think I was ever going to see you again.'

'So now I am here have you told Serena it's hands off time? Have you told her we're back together?'

'We had other more pressing issues to discuss.'

'So you haven't told her,' accused Megan, her eyes glinting. 'Damn you, Luigi, you'd better do it quickly, because if I take any more calls from her I'll fill her so full of home truths that she won't even want to work with you, never mind insinuating herself into your bed.'

Megan knew that she was getting too wound up for her

own good but she couldn't help it. She was afraid that everything was going to go pear-shaped, and she'd end up being even more hurt than before. And this time Charlotte would be hurt too. This was her main concern.

'I can assure you, Megan,' he said in a low growl, 'that you are my number one priority. Serena never has nor ever will enter the equation.'

He looked as though he wanted to kiss her, actually bowing his head and inching closer. Pulses began to race and Megan knew that if she hesitated it would be too late. With speed born of panic she flung open the door. 'I wish I could believe you. Goodnight, Luigi.' And she slammed it behind her.

Her heart raced as though she'd run a hundred-yard sprint. It would be so easy to fall back into their old ways, to become Luigi's wife again in every sense of the word. But it was too soon. He had to prove himself first. She must take control of her feelings, not give the slightest hint that she wanted him like she never had before. It was going to be hard but she had to do it, for the sake of their future.

Sleep didn't come easily. What was easy was remembering Luigi in bed beside her. The space felt empty. She felt empty. If they had nothing else in common she couldn't deny that they made a spectacular couple in bed.

Frequently she wandered into Charlotte's room to check that she was OK. She looked so beautiful and so innocent with not a care in the world, happy to be in this house with her father, and for her sake Megan was glad that she'd agreed to stay on.

When she went down to breakfast the next morning Megan was surprised to see Luigi seated at the table, the morning paper spread out in front of him, a steaming cup of coffee in his hand. Luigi was very much a coffee man.

He'd once told her that he'd had so much tea poured into him as a child that it had put him off it for life.

'Good morning.' He looked up with a warm smile. 'Did you sleep well?'

Should she lie and say yes, or tell the truth? Megan lied. 'Brilliantly well, thank you. And yourself?'

'Yes, I had a good night too.'

But she knew they were both politely lying. She was willing to bet that he'd tossed and turned the whole night as well, wishing they were together, reliving the magical moments they'd shared. Feeling stirred by them, feeling a hunger that was hard to dismiss.

Even as she'd walked into the room and their eyes met, Megan's senses had skidded out of control and she'd had to turn away quickly, making a big thing of helping Charlotte into her chair.

Charlotte chatted away to her father and Megan was able to take a firm hold of her dithering emotions. This was ridiculous. How could she live with Luigi and follow her own self-imposed rules feeling as she did? Why not share his bed? Because, came the severe answer, you'll be doubly hurt if it doesn't work. And that had to be the truth.

Not until Edwina had brought in their breakfast did Megan question Luigi. 'I thought you'd be at work. It's a quarter past eight. If I remember rightly you're normally at your desk by seven-thirty.'

'So you didn't believe me when I said I was going to change?' he asked with a mocking lift to an eyebrow.

His hair was neatly combed, his jaw clean-shaven and he smelt heavenly. For the life of her she couldn't remember the name of his cologne, but he had always used the same one for as long as she'd known him. To her it was an aphrodisiac and as she inhaled it she closed her eyes and dreamt of him making love to her.

'Is something wrong?' asked Luigi sharply.

'What? I'm sorry. No! Nothing! And, no, I didn't believe you. But I'm glad to see that you've kept your word.' He was wearing a white silk shirt, open at the throat, and she had an insane urge to touch his chest with her fingertips, to feel the strength of that muscular body, to—

'Megan?'

Again he brought her back to the present.

'Are you sure you've had enough sleep? You look as though you're in a trance. Shall I take the day off and look after Charlotte while—?'

'No!' she exclaimed strongly. 'There's nothing wrong with me. I was thinking about something, that's all. Mmm, this bacon smells good.'

As they ate she was aware of him watching her, and when Charlotte had finished and run away into the kitchen to 'help 'Wina' he said, 'Something's wrong, isn't it? I hope you're not having second thoughts, or should I say third? Because, make no bones about it, this is now your home.'

'I know,' Megan said quietly. 'You don't have to rub it in. I have no intention of leaving, not yet anyway.'

'By the way,' he said, as he poured himself yet another cup of coffee, Megan shaking her head when he offered her one, 'I've employed a nanny for Charlotte.'

'You've done what?' That really did wake her up and Megan bounced her hands off the table, her eyes flashing furiously. 'What have you done that for? I'm perfectly capable of looking after my own daughter.'

'Of course you are,' he said evenly. 'You've proved that, but wouldn't it be nice to have more time to yourself?'

'No, it wouldn't,' she slammed. 'You'd better ring her right now and tell her she's not wanted. You have no idea what a child needs. It's certainly not a stranger looking after her; her parents' time and love is far more important.' She was beside herself with rage. How could he do this without consulting her? Quite easily, came the answer. He was used to giving orders, used to organising. But she was not one of his employees and he wasn't going to tell her what to do.

'I happen to think that it's important for *us* to spend more time together,' he said, visibly containing his patience. 'We have a lot of catching up to do, Megan.'

'And how can we do that when you work all the hours God gave?' she snapped.

'Because I shall make time,' he retorted harshly, pushing himself to his feet and glaring down at her.

'Ha! That will be a first,' she thrust back. 'How long will it last, I wonder? One day? Two? A whole week at the most?' And she too sprang up from her chair.

'Things are different now I have a daughter,' he rasped, dark eyes glittering. 'I'm a family man now and I intend to take care of my family.'

'And hiring a nanny is part of that care?' she yelled. 'What if Charlotte doesn't like her? What if—?'

'We'll give it a try,' he interjected tersely, his fingers clenching as he fought for control. 'And that's the end of it.'

Megan flounced out of the room. Arguing with Luigi when he was in this mood got her nowhere, but she was fiercely determined not to give in. When the nanny arrived she would tell her in no uncertain terms that she wasn't needed. Luigi could say what he liked; Charlotte did not need a nanny. Not when she was at home all day to look after her. If Luigi wanted to spend more time at home he would have to put up with Charlotte as well, he wasn't getting rid of her that easily.

Was that it, she wondered, for all his fine words he found an excitable, energetic daughter too daunting? He didn't like his routine upset. A nanny would solve the problem. Another case of using the power of his money to get what he wanted. Megan spat fire as she sought her daughter in the kitchen. How dared he dictate? How dared he try to take over her life?

It was evening before she saw him again and her anger hadn't subsided. As soon as Charlotte was in bed she began her attack. 'I hope you've cancelled the nanny?'

'Why would I do that?' A harsh frown dragged his thick brows together.

'You mean you didn't listen to a word I said?' Megan's eyes flashed her fury. In fact her whole body grew stiff with rage and she battered her fists against his chest. 'Just because *you* can't handle Charlotte it doesn't mean *I* need help.'

In response he pulled her hard against him, his arms binding her so that she could no longer fight. 'I am doing this for *us*, not Charlotte.' His dark eyes pierced her own, sending a *frisson* of awareness through her despite the anger that she felt—or perhaps because of it! '*We* are the ones who need time,' he asserted strongly. 'We have a whole four years to catch up.'

'And you think that handing over *our* daughter to a complete stranger will help?' she questioned hotly. 'As far as I'm concerned there's nothing to talk about. I'm still convinced that I did the right thing.'

Luigi snorted his annoyance. 'If it were just you and me then I could perhaps understand. But I'll never be able to forgive you for depriving me of my daughter's first years.'

'I doubt you'd have seen much of her,' she scorned, struggling in vain to free herself. 'In case you've forgotten, your continual absence was the reason I walked out.'

'Dammit, Megan, why do you keep throwing that at me?' he charged, tightening his hold. 'What I want to know is why you never made me aware of it?'

'Oh, I did, believe me, many times,' she yelled into his face, her eyes flashing dramatically. 'You wouldn't listen, that was the problem. You were so wrapped up in your entrepreneurial world that nothing I said sank in. You assumed that making money was high on my list of priorities too. Well, let me tell you—' Her words were cut off by Luigi's mouth closing over hers. And in that moment Megan knew that she had lost.

CHAPTER SIX

LUIGI found it hard to accept that Megan was against him employing someone to look after Charlotte. It was the perfect solution. They needed to spend more time together, they needed to iron out the problems that had sent her fleeing; how could they do that with a three-year-old constantly demanding their attention?

He'd thought hard about their situation and had made up his mind that he would delegate more in order to give Megan his undivided attention. Admittedly he would like to be involved with the problems with the new software, and he'd like to keep his eye on the running of Gerards. But in truth he had staff who were more than capable of dealing with any situation.

He didn't pay good wages for nothing. He expected hard work and loyalty, and that was what he usually got. It was only his own desire to be involved in all aspects of his varied business interests that kept him going long hours. But now he was needed in another, more important, direction. Probably the most important one of his life. His whole future depended on it.

His arms became more possessive. Megan was his! She belonged to him for all time. He'd made mistakes but their future was transparently clear. The three of them were a family and nothing or no one was going to split them up. Employing a nanny was a necessity as far as he was concerned. He and Megan desperately needed time; they needed to renew their vows, to renew the love that had once bound them so firmly together.

On the day they met he'd fallen instantly in love and even if she hadn't let him drive her home with her dangerously overflowing bags of Christmas goodies he would have found some other way to get to know her. Maybe meeting her again at Christmas time was a good omen. The thought pleased him and he deepened his kiss, even more thrilled when Megan didn't resist.

She felt so good in his arms, her slender body moulding perfectly to his, and he silently prayed that she would let him back into her bed. He had tasted paradise and then been denied it. More than once in the endless dark hours he'd padded to her door, prepared to storm in and not take no for an answer. How he had turned around and returned to his room he didn't know. It had been sheer hell.

But thankfully she was weakening. The way she was kissing him now with complete abandonment, the way she moved her body suggestively against his, was all the encouragement he needed. He lifted her into his arms with the initial thought of carrying her up to bed, but then thought better of it and they ended up on the sofa instead.

'My beautiful Megan,' he whispered huskily into her ear. 'You've no idea how hard it's been having you in my house and not being allowed to touch you.'

'Don't talk,' she breathed, pulling his mouth down to hers and kissing him so passionately that he felt as though all his dreams were coming true. But suddenly Charlotte's scream cut through their pleasure.

They were both on their feet in an instant, Megan hurtling up the stairs in panic. He followed close behind. What had happened to his daughter? Had she fallen? Was she hurt? His heart thudded as he realised how deeply he had come to love this child in the few short days he'd known her.

Charlotte was sitting straight up in bed, her eyes wide and staring. 'She's asleep,' said Megan, slowing her hectic race. 'She's dreaming.'

'Does she often do this, dream with her eyes open?' asked Luigi in concern. It looked weird to him.

'Only when something's upset her. It's some kind of nightmare, I think. It's always the same.'

As they watched Charlotte's body relaxed, her eyes closed and she gave a half smile as she curled up beneath the bedcovers again.

Megan leaned over her and gave her a gentle kiss. 'I try not to wake her because then she doesn't remember.'

Luigi frowned. 'What could have upset her?'

Megan shrugged and straightened the quilt. 'Maybe she heard us arguing. She's a sensitive little soul and we didn't keep our voices very low, did we?'

Luigi shook his head. 'We were too far away.' But a shadow of guilt made him uneasy. He had a lot to learn about children. 'Will she be all right if we leave her?'

'I'm going to stay in my room just in case,' declared Megan. 'Alone!' she added warningly.

Luigi compressed his lips. 'We have unfinished business.'

'That was a mistake,' retorted Megan on a loud whisper.

'Like marrying me was a mistake?' He couldn't help himself. He'd been so confident that tonight was the night they'd both realise that they couldn't sleep apart, and to have it all snatched away from him because Charlotte had had a bad dream drove him crazy.

'Since you put it like that, yes.' Her eyes were cool on his, her earlier passion gone, melting as quickly as the snowflakes outside.

'I think you're lying,' he snarled. 'You're afraid to admit it but you still care for me.'

'In your dreams, Mister,' she hissed.

'Then why, when I kiss you, do you melt in my arms? Why do you return my kiss with so much passion that it makes a lie of everything you're saying? Tell me that, dear wife of mine. Look me in the eye and tell me you have no feelings for me.'

Megan woke with a start. She'd been dreaming about Luigi and had the strangest feeling that he was standing beside her. But the room was empty. Even Charlotte hadn't yet stirred. She switched on the bedside lamp and looked at the clock. Almost half past seven! It was unusual for her daughter to still be asleep. Usually she crept into her bed at around six and they both dozed for another hour.

She rolled out of bed and padded across to the window. It was dark, and all was still and cold and eerily white outside from a further fall of snow. Then she crossed to the adjoining door and opened it wider. What she hadn't expected to see was Luigi sitting in a chair beside Charlotte's bed holding her hand. They were both asleep.

For at least two minutes Megan stood there watching and wondering. Had her instinct been right when she'd thought he was beside her bed? She didn't like the thought that he'd crept into her room in the middle of the night. He could have slipped in beside her and she wouldn't have known! Had that been his intention and then he'd had second thoughts and decided to sit with his daughter instead?

Last night she'd declared that she had no feelings for

him, that he managed to arouse her sexually but that was all. She'd even looked him straight in the eye as she'd said it. Because it was the truth. She didn't love him any more. *She didn't!*

Suddenly she realised that Luigi had opened his eyes and was watching her. 'What are you doing?' she asked in a fierce whisper.

Gently he let his daughter's hand go and moved stiffly across the room towards her. Megan shut the adjoining door and glared at him as she waited for his answer.

'Charlotte cried out again,' he informed her.

Megan was horrified that she hadn't heard. In fact she found it hard to believe. 'Are you sure?'

'I wouldn't have been sitting there if I wasn't,' he informed her, stretching his arms above his head and yawning widely. His silk dressing gown fell open, revealing a pair of black boxer shorts and a tanned bare chest.

Megan's heartbeats quickened.

'She didn't wake but I thought she ought to have company and, as you looked so beautiful and comfortable in your sleep,' he growled, 'I didn't want to disturb you.'

'You should have woken me,' she tossed stormily. 'It's my place to be with her.'

'Not any longer,' he said with a warning light in his eyes. 'We share responsibility now.'

The days of sharing with Luigi had long since gone. Luigi was his own man, doing only what he wanted to do. And at this moment he thought that sitting holding Charlotte's hand made him look good. Would he be as quick to be at her side if she were throwing up? Somehow Megan doubted it.

'We *share*?' she echoed, 'and yet you've gone to the trouble of employing a nanny. How hypocritical is that?'

'It's different; it's a necessity.'

'So you keep saying. I don't happen to think so. I like looking after my daughter; perhaps you're not aware of that. I don't want a stranger doing it for me.'

'I've said all I'm saying on that matter,' he retorted sharply and headed for the door.

By the time he'd gone Charlotte had woken and when they went down to breakfast Luigi had left. 'He said he won't be more than a couple of hours,' informed William, who had been entrusted with the message. 'Something urgent cropped up.'

As it always did, thought Megan bitterly.

Amazingly, though, within the two hours he was back. Accompanying him was a smart young woman with long blonde hair. She was tall and slim and very good-looking. Serena, thought Megan, her hackles instantly rising. How dared he bring her here?

She and Charlotte were outside building yet another snowman and Luigi was all smiles as he approached them. 'Megan, let me introduce Kate Swift, Charlotte's nanny. Kate, my wife, Megan, and this is my daughter,' he added proudly.

Megan knew she must look stupid with her mouth falling open and it was with a great deal of reluctance that she took Kate's outstretched hand. 'I hadn't realised you were starting today,' she said, trying to smile, but unable to keep a terse note out of her voice.

'I thought it a good idea,' explained Luigi.

And Megan knew why. He didn't want Charlotte spoiling their lovemaking again. With a nanny on call twenty-four hours a day it would clear the way for him. The selfish swine! But if he thought she was going to leave her precious daughter totally in the care of someone else he was gravely mistaken.

'And this is Charlotte?' Kate stooped down to the child's level. 'Hello, Charlotte. What a grand snowman! Have you built it?'

But Charlotte had her thumb stuck in her mouth and clung to Megan's hand, looking curiously at the smiling woman.

'She's always shy with strangers,' explained Megan, a cool note still in her voice.

'I think we should go indoors and let Kate settle in,' said Luigi cheerfully.

'Charlotte and I need to finish our snowman,' said Megan. She was furious with Luigi. He had no right bringing that woman here without telling her first. She had thought, or at least hoped, that she'd convinced him that she didn't want anyone else looking after Charlotte. It was a crazy idea. What the hell was she supposed to do all day while Kate took over?

'Who's that lady?' asked Charlotte as soon as they had disappeared into the house.

Megan drew in a deep breath and paused a moment before answering, 'She's come to help Mummy look after you, sweetheart.'

'I don't want her, I want you,' Charlotte said almost on a shout. 'And Daddy,' she added after a moment's thought.

'You'll still have us, don't worry, sweetheart. But sometimes, if Daddy and I have to go out, then Kate will look after you.' It was the best explanation she could think of.

'Will she play with me?'

'Of course.'

'Will she build a snowman, and play snowballs?'

'I'm sure she will.'

'Will she read me bedtime stories?'

Megan's heart began to break. 'Sometimes, perhaps, but that's my job. That's the best, don't you think, when you're tucked up in bed and I read to you. That's our special time of day.'

Charlotte nodded her satisfaction and then began to play in the snow.

By the end of the day Charlotte had accepted Kate and Megan had to grudgingly admit that Kate was very good with her daughter. It didn't alter the fact, though, that she resented her presence, and she fully intended telling Luigi exactly what she thought.

Once Charlotte was in bed Kate retired. She'd made a fuss about Megan wanting to bathe Charlotte and put her to bed, declaring that it was part of her job, but Megan had been adamant.

Luigi had provided the new nanny with her own sitting room and bedroom, opposite Charlotte's room, so that she was on hand should she be needed quickly. This was something else Megan didn't approve of. Why should Kate need to be so near?

Megan was silent over dinner, her anger simmering away inside her, trying to decide how best to tackle him.

'Why don't you spit it out?' asked Luigi harshly. There was fire in his eyes too.

'You know I didn't want Charlotte to have a nanny. Was that why you presented me with a *fait accompli?*'

He shrugged laconically. 'Don't you like Kate?'

'That's nothing to do with it,' she shot back. 'You went behind my back. You knew how I felt and yet you didn't even have the decency to talk it over with me.'

'We'd already discussed it.'

'You mean you told me what you'd decided. My feelings didn't count. You're a rat, Luigi. I don't know what I ever saw in you. And I honestly don't know what I'm doing here. Second to marrying you it's the biggest mistake of my life.' She pushed her plate away and jumped up from the table. 'I can't even face eating with you.'

She heard Luigi's swift intake of disbelief before he was on his feet too, his hands on her shoulders, fingers merciless. 'You don't mean that.'

'Don't I?' she rasped, looking angrily into the hard darkness of his eyes.

'You know deep in your heart that it's for the best,' he thrust fiercely. 'We need this time together. In fact, once Charlotte's got used to Kate, it will do us good to go away for a few days.'

'And leave my daughter?' she screeched.

'Our daughter,' he corrected harshly. 'And don't think I'd dream of leaving her if I wasn't sure that she'd be in good hands. But we need time together, the two of us, alone, completely. We need to sort out our lives.'

'And you'll arrange that, without consulting me yet again?' she blazed. 'I think not. I think you're under a great big delusion. You think that now you've got me in your house you can do what the hell you like. It's not true. I'm tougher than you think. I've had to be. If you don't believe me just wait and see. If you carry on in this vein you might find one day that I've disappeared again.'

The grip on her shoulders tightened so much that a sharp pain seared through her bones. 'Do that at your peril,' he threatened menacingly. 'What I'm doing is for your good, for *our* good. How the hell are we supposed to get back on an even keel with a child at our heels all the time?'

'*A child?*' Megan screamed. 'Is that how you see Charlotte? A mere child, a nuisance! How dare you? You make her sound like a stranger. She's your flesh and blood, Luigi. You should be delirious with pleasure. You should be glad to have her around. You should be getting to know her better.'

'And I think,' he grated harshly, 'that we should work on our own relationship before Charlotte's. Of course I love my daughter; she's brought life to the house. She's a beautiful, intelligent little girl and I'm proud of her. But we need to get our own lives in order.'

'That's rich, coming from you,' she riposted. 'You were the one who let our marriage down. And, to be perfectly honest, I can't see you changing. Your answer to everything is to pay someone to do your dirty work. Including looking after your daughter. How sad is that?' And finally, with strength born of desperation, she managed to tear free. But she didn't leave the room. Instead she stood a few feet away, glaring at Luigi like an enraged tigress.

His eyes narrowed, becoming two glittering slits that reflected the light from the lamps. And his whole body was tense with a rage he was doing his level best to control. Not that Megan cared whether he controlled it or not. She was past caring what Luigi felt. All she was concerned about was her darling daughter's welfare.

'I think,' he said fiercely, 'that you're blowing this thing up out of all proportion. It will do you good to have more time to yourself.'

'And there'll be lots of that,' she retorted hostilely, 'because you'll still be working all the hours God gave. You're all talk, Luigi. How could you possibly take time off? Everything would collapse if you weren't at the helm.'

Her sarcasm wasn't lost on him. She saw the muscles clench in his jaw, the way his mouth went even straighter and grimmer, and it was a second or two before he answered. And when he did his voice was deadly calm. 'I've said I'll take you away, Megan, and that's exactly what I intend to do.'

'And if I don't want to come? Charlotte's never been parted from me. I wouldn't leave her if I thought she'd be upset.'

He brushed her doubts away. 'We'll give her time to get used to Kate. She comes with the highest recommendation; I don't think we have a problem.'

'And no doubt you're paying her the highest wage,' she retorted. 'I truly never expected that you'd turn out like this. Money, money, money, all the time. I must have been insane to marry you.'

'Is it a crime to want to better oneself?' he asked icily.

'Of course not, but there's a limit. You're taking things a step too far.'

'In your eyes, not mine.'

'So you're happy here in this mausoleum of a home? You enjoy having other people run around after you, pandering to your every whim? Is that the pleasure money brings? It doesn't seem like pleasure to me.'

'So tell me, Megan.' He cocked his head on one side and looked at her consideringly. 'What does pleasure you?'

Her cheeks flushed beneath that knowing stare, and her heart faltered as she realised that she had left herself wide open.

He moved purposefully towards her. 'Don't tell me,' he said on a low growl. 'Let me show you.'

Before she could even draw breath she was in his arms, her mouth opening of its own volition beneath the persuasive power of his. Megan knew that she ought to protest— loudly, volubly; she ought to push him away, show him that actions like this got him nowhere. But, fool that she was, she let her senses take over.

She enjoyed the thrill of his hard, sexy body against hers. She revelled in the feelings he aroused deep within her. She wanted more. She wanted all of him! The thought set off alarm bells in her head but she chose to ignore them. Luigi had talked about catching up on the years they'd spent apart, but it was their times in bed that she'd missed. Missed without really knowing it. Was it any wonder that she'd kept herself a man-free zone? No other man was good enough. No other man could possibly arouse her to this extent. They were soulmates as far as good sex was concerned.

Megan oughtn't to have taunted him. Kissing her at this moment in time was the worst thing he could possibly do—except that she was so damned gorgeous how could he resist? Which begged the question, why hadn't he made more of an effort to find her? Luigi knew that he could never come up with an answer. He'd been a fool. It was as simple as that. A blind fool, who thought that immersing himself in his work was the answer to everything.

And now he had a lot of making up to do. He was fully aware that it was going to be a long, hard slog and that he mustn't go too quickly—even if at times like this she actually seemed to welcome his advances. It was pure sex, she'd said, and although he didn't want to believe her he sometimes felt that she was right. And this was one of those occasions.

With reluctance he drew away. He stepped back a pace and felt virtuous that she looked surprised and a teeny bit disappointed. No, hugely disappointed. She was totally aroused, he could tell by her flushed cheeks and shining eyes, and if he had pushed his luck he could have taken her to bed. Which he wanted to! Very much so! His testosterone levels had risen to danger point. But it was good that he had stopped. It would show her that sex wasn't the only thing he wanted from their relationship.

'I think we ought to finish our dinner,' he said gruffly.

'I'm not hungry.'

Nor was he—except for this woman, his wife. He clamped his lips and nodded, only the slightest movement of his head. Megan didn't even notice. But that was what she was, his wife. She belonged to him. She could run but he would never divorce her. One day they would be a happy and contented couple again. With perhaps another child to keep Charlotte company. It was only a matter of time.

Megan went to bed with a heavy heart. Luigi was doing his best and she appreciated that, but in her eyes it wasn't good enough. And letting him make love to her was no answer either; it distorted her judgement, it reminded her of all that had been good in their marriage. It made her forget the long hours of neglect. So, although she had felt bereft when he backed away, she was now glad of it, and determined not to let herself be swayed into such a position again. Easy to say but difficult to do! Even the thought of kissing Luigi had her aching inside and she wasn't sure that she could be strong enough to deny him.

But she would give it a good try. Luigi needed to reform; he needed to put his wife and daughter before his business interests. And when he did that—then perhaps their marriage would stand a chance.

His idea of taking her away for a few days was a sound one in principle. In fact it would be heaven—if it weren't for Charlotte, and the fact that Megan knew unequivocally that once they were back he would revert to his old ways. Who was it who said that a leopard never changed its spots? Luigi would never change. Working was his way of life; his wife and now his child came second. They always would.

She was almost asleep when her door slowly opened. At first she thought she was dreaming when she saw Luigi's shadowy shape in the doorway, but as he began to make his way softly over to her bed she sat bolt upright. Her heart stampeded as her need for him rose like a phoenix from the ashes.

But fear overrode her desire. 'What the hell are you doing here?' Her voice was low but shrill and there was panic inside her. He was a danger to her system—and he probably knew it. He knew that relaxed in bed she would be at her lowest ebb, and it would be easy to take advantage.

'There's something I need to ask you.' He came to a halt at her side and looked fiercely down. And Megan didn't see desire, she didn't see a deep-seated need of her body, instead she saw something that sent a chill through her entire system.

CHAPTER SEVEN

'I'VE just discovered that you haven't been entirely truthful with me,' Luigi spat.

Megan frowned. 'What do you mean?' She had no idea what he was talking about. And she'd never seen him look at her so coldly or accusingly. It set her teeth on edge and made goose-bumps rise all over her body.

'The fact that you indulged in an affair with another man and lied to me about it,' he shot at her harshly.

'What?' she shrieked, jumping up from the bed. 'You're not making sense. Who, for pity's sake, am I supposed to have slept with?' She dragged her dressing gown on over her nightie and hugged it closely around her. 'Where did you conjure up that piece of fiction?'

'Straight from the horse's mouth, if you must know,' he thundered.

Megan shook her head. 'This is nonsense.'

'I knew you'd say that,' he scorned. 'I was expecting it.'

'So why don't you tell me who's made these accusations?' she asked him coldly, an icy shiver beginning to take over. It was all she could do to keep herself still.

'Your dear friend, Jake.'

'*Jake?*' Megan echoed dazedly. 'You have to be joking.

In any case, when did you speak to him? Jenny hasn't rung to say they're back.'

'They are, I assure you. I phoned them myself.'

'Why?' she questioned loudly.

'I needed to make sure she wasn't out of pocket with you moving out so suddenly.'

'And you spoke to Jake, and he told you that he and I had had an affair, is that what you're saying?' Megan couldn't comprehend. Why would Jake make such a statement when it wasn't true?

'He hinted that you'd been friends before Jenny came on the scene, and the emphasis he put on the word "friends" made me realise what he was trying to tell me.'

'So he didn't put it in as many words?'

'He didn't need to. I got the message.'

It was true; she had known Jake before Jenny did. She had worked with him when she first came to London, and he'd sort of taken her under his wing. But she hadn't had any kind of relationship with him, even though he would have liked to. She hadn't felt ready to commit to any man. One day he'd gone back to the flat with her to borrow a book and she'd been delighted when he and Jenny struck up a close friendship.

'Why should it bother you that I might have seen other men during our separation?' she asked him coolly, at the same time thinking that this could work in her favour. Luigi had had other girls, she knew, but he seemed incensed when it came to her doing the same. This could be a way to keep him at a distance.

'Because you're my woman,' he snarled, practically bouncing on his feet. His dark eyes glittered in the light from the bedside lamp, and his face was angular and savage—and gorgeously handsome.

Megan shook the thought away. Luigi was her number one enemy. She must remember that. She must never see him as an expert lover, as a man who could melt her bones by a mere glance or a touch. He had never treated her fairly, not once in all the years of their marriage. He was self-centred and egotistical. She dismissed the fact that he was an excellent provider and an expert businessman. It was the unadulterated love of a good man that she desired. And love wasn't high on Luigi's list of priorities. In fact she doubted it even existed.

'I am not your woman,' she told him tersely. 'You gave up all rights to me when you chose work over your marriage.'

'I did it for *us!*' he exclaimed loudly.

'So you keep saying. But it wasn't what I wanted.'

'And did Jake Whatever-his-name-is give you what you wanted?' he demanded fiercely.

'That's my business.' She saw the angry glitter harden in his eyes and his body swayed dangerously towards her. But she stood her ground, her eyes fierce in their determination, even though there was a part of her that couldn't dismiss the sensations playing on her nerve-ends—excitement and hatred bundled into one.

'And I think it's my business now to remind you, in a very personal way, that I don't want any other man to touch you ever again.' They were so close that Megan could feel his breath on her face, feel the warmth of his body, and she could even smell the male sexiness that had at one time driven her insane. 'You *are* my woman,' he continued grimly. 'You can deny it all you like, but you belong to me for the rest of your life.'

If that wasn't a warning she didn't know what was. *For the rest of her life!* In her present frame of mind it sounded like a death sentence and she wanted to lash out, to pound her fists on his hard, muscular chest, to kick his shins, to let him know in no uncertain terms that he was mistaken.

But she was afraid to make too much noise in case she woke Charlotte. So she maintained a reasonable decorum. 'Carry on like that and I really will divorce you,' she said quietly. 'Marriages aren't built on threats, nor on absentee husbands. And if you can't live with the fact that you *believe* I've had an affair with Jake then I'll willingly move out.'

'*No!*'

The boom of his voice sent her eyes fluttering towards Charlotte's door, fortunately closed. Sometimes she left it open, but tonight she'd been reading and was afraid the light might waken her daughter. She thanked her lucky stars now for her foresight.

'I've told you, I will never let you go.'

'Unless you change your ways you won't be able to hold me,' she declared vehemently. 'Threats won't work.'

'I'll threaten you all I like,' he snarled, 'since you don't seem to be prepared to even meet me halfway.'

'Meet you, when you are the one laying down the rules?' she questioned heatedly. 'You are the one who insisted I stay here. You are the one who insisted on employing a nanny for Charlotte. You are the one who's insisting we go away for a few days. My opinion has never counted.'

'Because I know what's good for you.'

Megan's anger boiled over. 'There you go again. When are you going to get it through your thick skull that a happy marriage means give and take? All you do is take, and I'm heartily fed up with it. Change that attitude and we might get somewhere.'

She watched as his mouth folded into a grim line and his eyes narrowed until she could see nothing through the slits of his lids. A quiver of unease tracked its way through her limbs. It looked as though she'd gone too far. Yet he deserved it. Why shouldn't she toss him a few home truths?

'I'd appreciate it if you'd meet me halfway, Megan.'

It was not the response she'd expected and although it was delivered in hard, terse tones she couldn't help feeling a twinge of guilt. She dismissed it immediately. Guilt had no place to play in this scenario. Not on her part anyway. Luigi was the one at fault—every inch of the way.

She had thought that meeting his daughter would soften him up, but that hadn't happened. He was no nearer to being a caring husband or father than he had been all those years ago. He was in charge and he expected everyone to jump at his command. Well, not this girl!

'Why should I?' she asked with a toss of her head. 'Why should I subject my daughter to a tyrant of a father?'

'Tyrant?' he exploded. 'Is that how you see me?'

'All the time.'

He closed his eyes and his fingers curled into tight fists, and Megan had the feeling that it was taking all his self-control not to lash out at her. She was tired of this confrontation. She wanted him to go. He had come here ready for a fight and because she hadn't caved in and eaten humble pie he was still spoiling for one.

She wouldn't give him that pleasure.

'Fortunately Charlotte doesn't see it that way,' she added. 'Perhaps because she hasn't been here long enough and you're on your best behaviour in front of her.'

Luigi snorted derisively. 'You have no idea what you're talking about. You're blinded by hatred. In fact you're the one with the problem. If you'd jump down off your high horse occasionally you'd see how much I've changed.'

Megan gave a tight, brittle laugh. 'Then I must be blind.

Have we finished this conversation? I really would like to get some sleep.' Not that she expected to drop off now. She was far too uptight.

'Maybe it is finished, but not satisfactorily,' he barked, swinging on his heel and heading for the door.

'You mean that it hurt when I didn't deny having a fling with Jake?' she taunted. 'I wouldn't worry about it if I were you. I'm not worrying about the girls you bedded while I was busy bringing up your daughter. We were free agents at the time. Why drag up the past?'

Again his mouth thinned but to give him his due he didn't retaliate; he simply wrenched open the door and stepped smartly outside. She half-expected him to slam it, was thankful when he didn't. She didn't want Charlotte or even Kate wondering why he was storming out of her room.

The thought occurred to her that Kate might not know they slept in separate rooms. Had Luigi told her anything about their circumstances, or did she think they were a normal happily married couple? It could be embarrassing if she ever came in to see to Charlotte and saw that Megan slept alone.

Luigi had been spitting fire when he sought Megan out. He had phoned her friend on the spur of the moment, not really knowing whether she was back from France. Jake had answered. And when Luigi stated his business he had gone into a long tribute to Megan. So much so that Luigi had begun to gain the impression that more had gone on between them than Megan had ever admitted. He'd felt an indescribable jealousy. The very thought of another man touching his wife was sickeningly abhorrent and he'd been prepared to shake the truth out of Megan.

And now when he thought back on their conversation

he realised that he hadn't won at all. Megan was tougher than he'd realised and she had fought back with admirable qualities. He still didn't know whether she'd actually slept with Jake and the thought drove him crazy.

So much so that he couldn't sleep. In the end he dragged on a tartan dressing gown over his boxer shorts, went downstairs to his den and sat at his computer. There was work that needed to be done but, dammit, he couldn't do that either. He kept seeing images of a fired-up Megan as she stood before him.

How he had fought the urge to pull her hard against him he didn't know. He'd wanted to forget everything Jake had told him and make love to her. With her hair tousled and her face flushed, and nothing on beneath her cotton nightdress, his virulent male hormones had sprung into life. He loved Megan so much that it tore him apart when she rejected him. Was he really as bad as she painted?

It was true that no one ever saw themselves as other people did, but a tyrant? Always taking, never giving? He wasn't like that. The presents he'd bought both her and Charlotte should have proved it. And she had this huge house to live in, no more worries about rent. He was prepared to give her anything she wanted. He'd even cut down on his working hours; hadn't she noticed that?

The more he thought about it the more confused he became. He picked up the whisky bottle and poured himself a generous measure, tossing it down his throat in one swallow before refilling it. This time he set it on the desk in front of him, fingering the cut-glass, twisting it absently round and round. But the more he thought about the situation the more he failed to understand it and fury rose once more inside him. He gulped down the rest of the whisky and in a fit of rage threw the glass at the fireplace, shattering it into a thousand tiny pieces.

The next moment his door was pushed open and there stood Megan, pale-faced and questioning, still in her nightdress and dressing gown. *With nothing on underneath!* This was the first thought that registered. The second was, what was she doing here? Why wasn't she in bed? And his third, perhaps she'd had a change of heart, realised that she'd been too hard on him, and had come to make amends.

His entire body throbbed in anticipation.

Megan looked from him to the fragments of glass in the hearth and then back again, a faint frown dragging her brows together. 'So you're still angry about Jake?'

Damn! She wasn't supposed to have said that. He felt his sudden hope draining away. 'What are you doing here?' he enquired gruffly.

'I was on my way to the kitchen to heat some milk.'

'Your conscience troubling you?' he sneered. He couldn't help himself. His optimism had been so miserably dashed.

'Not as much as yours, obviously,' she riposted, backing away from the doorway, ready to carry on her journey.

'Wait!' he said, though he didn't know why. He wanted her company and yet he knew it would be volatile. But better that than nothing.

She looked boldly and questioningly in his direction. 'For what? More of what you've just put me through? No, thank you.' And this time she walked away.

But Luigi wasn't prepared to let her go. He couldn't get through this night without her. 'Megan, please.'

She faltered and stopped.

'Come and talk to me.'

'Why should I?'

'It's silly us both being wide awake. We may as well keep each other company.'

'Not if you're going to pick another fight.' She half turned towards him but still looked prepared to flee.

He held up his hands. 'Truce.'

'How can I believe you? You already have me hung, drawn and quartered. Why should I escape more misery?'

'Because I don't feel like my own company at this moment.' He was exposing his feelings in a way he never had before. He always liked to give the image that he was in complete control—which he usually was. It was only Megan who managed to instil doubt into him—doubt and despair.

'You mean you might throw a few more glasses? Is it an image of me that you're throwing them at or disgust with yourself?'

He winced, but refused to give her the pleasure of seeing how accurate her second guess was. 'Perhaps it's a bad idea. I wasn't intending it to be a re-run of what happened upstairs. I simply thought we might both enjoy some company. But if it's too much for you…' He saw her hesitate, the doubt in her eyes, then the reluctant decision that he might be right.

'Very well,' she answered quietly, 'but I'd still like some hot milk. How about you?'

On top of whisky! But if it helped keep her at his side… 'I'd like that, shall I—?'

'Come and help? No thanks! I'll be back in a few minutes.'

He watched her walk along the corridor, her behind swaying seductively with each step that she took. She walked like a model, every inch of her alerting his senses to such a degree that he began to question the perverseness that had made him invite her into his sanctum. He wouldn't be able to touch her, he knew that, there was a mile-wide gap between them that would be difficult, if not impossible, to bridge. Not in a few minutes, or even hours. Days, weeks maybe, but he wasn't that patient.

To him it was simple. They resumed marital relations and the rest would follow. It was Megan who was making progress difficult, finding problems when there were none. He would never understand her.

In the five minutes it took her to heat milk and make their drinks he'd decided that they needed to have a real heart to heart. It was the only way they would be able to solve their problems. And probably now, in the middle of the night, was the very best time. No Charlotte to interrupt, no phone calls, nothing except the two of them—together.

Hunger for her crept through every one of his strong male veins. How he was going to sit there, knowing that she was as naked as the day she was born beneath her enchanting white nightie, laced from waist to throat with a Christmas-red ribbon, and do nothing about it he didn't know. It would be the worst form of torture.

She returned with their drinks on a tray, together with a plate of home-made biscuits which he knew would choke him if he attempted to eat one. What he wanted to do was suck one of Megan's nipples into his mouth. She always tasted so beautiful and reacted so wantonly. He wanted to suck and bite and tease until she was putty in his hands. He wanted to feel her softly scented body close to him, he wanted to mould her with his palms, feel every curve and contour; he wanted to touch her most intimate places, feel her moistness, make her as ready for him as he was for her.

But he knew he couldn't.

She was out of bounds.

For the moment!

But soon…

Megan nibbled on a biscuit, sitting in the armchair opposite him where he couldn't possibly touch her, but he could look… It was warm in the room. He had stoked up the fire and it burned brightly in the grate. Her purple dressing gown was undone, the ribbon on her nightdress beckoning his fingers to untie the bow and unlace it. Lord, he wanted to look at her—she was his wife, after all. Instead she was covered up as primly as a nun.

He picked up his mug of malted milk and cradled it in his palms. It was absolutely no compensation for her temptingly full breasts. He felt compelled to close his eyes so that he needn't look at her.

'Are you tired now? Shall I go?'

Her question had his lids jerking open. 'Not at all. I was simply thinking.'

'About what? Us?'

He shrugged. 'Does it matter when you're determined that—?'

'I'm not determined about anything,' she forestalled him.

'I don't see any sign of you wishing to kiss and make up.'

'That's because a lot of water's gone under the bridge. Before we kiss we talk. We have to resolve our differences. It's the only way.'

'I'm trying.'

Megan raised her beautifully shaped brows. 'You could have fooled me.'

Something red shot in front of his eyes and he was ready to blast. It was only with an extreme effort that he managed to exercise caution and say calmly, 'Perhaps you're not really looking. You have it so firmly fixed in your mind that I'm the baddie in all of this that you're missing the improvements.'

'Spell them out to me.'

He didn't want to do that. It wasn't the answer. 'If you can't see them then perhaps I'm wasting my time.'

'I have noticed,' she said with slow consideration, 'that you don't spend quite so much time at work. But I assumed it was because of the Christmas holidays. It doesn't really prove anything.'

His breath whistled thinly through his teeth. 'Did I ever take time off at Christmas?' He couldn't help the sharpness of his tone.

'The first year we were married you did. We had a wonderful Christmas together.' Her eyes lit up as she spoke and he saw a glimpse of the girl he had first met. The girl who had ensnared him in an invisible net that could never be broken. 'But after that,' she went on, 'you only took Christmas Day off. Even then you were a grouch.'

That was because his mind was always connected to whatever money-spinning idea he was working on. Looking back, he could see that perhaps he had been a little unfair on Megan—but not as much as she was making out. 'So surely you can see,' he pointed out, his tone strong and firm, 'that I'm doing my level best to spend more time with you.'

'And how long will it last?' she asked caustically.

'With your co-operation, if you don't constantly raise your hackles whenever I'm around, for ever.' He saw the way her brows rose ever so slightly, the disbelief in her perfectly shaped grey eyes. 'I'm serious. I want this to work, Megan. You are my whole life. Without you it has no meaning.'

Disbelief gave way to surprise, her eyes widening as they remained steadily on his. 'You've never said anything like that before.'

'I didn't feel I had to. I thought you knew.'

'I know nothing unless you tell me,' she insisted.

Not that he loved her? How could that be? He didn't find

it easy to say the words, but surely she knew? Why else would he want her back? He took a long, slow drink from his mug, watching her over the rim as he did so. He could prove to her in bed exactly how much he loved her—if she would only let him. Dared he suggest it?

He didn't think so.

She was just as likely to slap him across the face. But even that contact would be better than the distance that separated them. It felt like a mile instead of a couple of feet.

Megan sipped her milk too, avoiding his eyes, staring absently into the flickering flames of the fire. She looked so beautiful sitting there, the glow from the coals warming her face, softening the shadows. He could imagine her in just such a position breast-feeding her baby. He had missed that! He had missed everything to do with Charlotte's birth and her first important years. He hadn't seen her learn to walk or talk, her first teeth coming through, her first word—which might have been 'Daddy' if he'd been there! Instead she'd never known what it was like to have a father.

Bitterness crept in and he began to wonder whether it had been such a good idea to invite Megan to sit with him. He didn't want a confrontation, but that was exactly how he felt. *So much he had missed!* And it was all her fault! He clattered his mug down on the table.

Megan followed suit. 'I'm feeling sleepy now,' she said, although he knew she was lying.

'I think I might go to bed too,' he declared. This wasn't how he had wanted it to end but it looked as though he had no choice.

'I'll leave you to make sure the fire's safe. Goodnight, Luigi.'

'Goodnight, Megan.'

So formal! No kiss, no touch, no sign that they meant

anything to each other, and yet he would stake everything he owned that her body craved his just as much as his did hers.

Perhaps he should kiss her, a gentle peck on the forehead, nothing more, just enough to let her know that he cared. But already it was too late; she had left the room and he could hear her running lightly up the stairs.

When he followed later his footsteps were much slower and heavier.

CHAPTER EIGHT

WHEN Megan woke the day was bright and sunny—and Charlotte's room was empty! It took her a second or two to remember that there was now a nanny to attend to her daughter's needs. It didn't please her. She enjoyed cuddling her sleepy-headed daughter first thing in the morning, feeling the heat of her skin, ruffling her already tousled hair. It was a mother-child thing and she didn't like the experience being taken from her.

Something else that she hated Luigi for!

She showered and dressed in a red sweater and black ski pants and went downstairs to find her daughter. Instead she found Luigi—in the breakfast room, his empty plate in front of him and a cup of coffee in his hand. 'Good morning.' He gave her a smile that sent an electric tingle down her spine.

Careful, she warned, don't fall into his trap. He was expert at seducing her senses. She had felt it last night; she had wanted to stay with him in his den and let him make love to her in front of the fire. So much she had wanted it. His needs had been her needs. She hadn't lived with him without being able to tell when he desired her. And, despite all the harsh things that she'd said to him, she had wanted him too.

But it wasn't in her plan of things. Before anything like that happened again she needed to be convinced that he'd reformed. Not only fewer hours at work but he needed to love his daughter in the way a child needed to be loved. Armfuls of presents were not the answer. She was still determined to take most of them back to the store, the ones he'd given her as well. She couldn't be bought; she wasn't a piece of baggage.

'What's going through that mind of yours? That frown's enough to frighten away the fiercest predator.' There was lazy amusement in his voice and it was good to see him looking so relaxed. Usually at this time of the morning he was eating a piece of toast while he fixed his tie—either that or he had already left. Perhaps he *was* turning over a new leaf.

'It is? Then I guess you're the predator as you're the only person in the room.'

'And you're my prey?' He looked pleased at the thought.

'I think not. Is the coffee still hot?' She was aware of his eyes on her breasts where they pushed against the thin wool of her sweater. His examination made them go taut with expectation, her nipples peaking, and the rest of her body filling with tingling warmth.

'Amy's going to bring you in some tea.'

'That's good of her.' She sat down quickly. This immediate reaction was unexpected. She even felt slightly breathless. It was madness. How could she keep up her campaign, feeling as she did?

'What would you like to eat?' Luigi pushed himself easily up from the table and strode to the heated tray on the sideboard, lifting lids on the silver dishes. 'Bacon? Sausage? Tomatoes? Mushrooms? Eggs? Some of each?'

He wore grey worsted trousers that fitted snugly over his hips, and a yellow cashmere sweater. It was a colour she'd never seen him in before. It suited his dark complexion. As she watched him peering into each dish in turn it occurred to her that she was studying him in exactly the same way as he had looked at her earlier, and she turned her head away. 'Toast and marmalade will be fine, thank you,' she announced primly.

'You're going to let this good food go to waste? Is that really all you want?'

'You know I never eat much in the morning. On the other hand, perhaps you don't. You were always in too much of a hurry to sit and have breakfast with me.' Her tone was deliberately sharp. It annoyed her that he was still able to arouse her without doing anything.

'I imagine that happens in most working families,' he said. 'But all that's changed. You no longer work. I don't have to go in so early. There's no reason in the world why we shouldn't sit and have breakfast together every morning.' He was back in his chair, pushing the toast rack and marmalade and butter dishes closer towards her.

'Pardon me,' she said, 'but I haven't given up my job yet. I'm still on Christmas leave.'

A brow rose. 'I forgot to tell you; I rang your firm and told them that you wouldn't be going back.'

'What?' Megan's eyes flashed outrage. He'd gone over her head again. 'You had no right. In any case, how did you know where I worked?'

'I made it my business to find out.' He didn't look in the least apologetic.

'Jenny told you—or Jake. Was it him?' She'd kill him when she next saw him.

'Does it matter who?'

It mattered to her. Very much! Where was her friends' sense of loyalty? She was trapped now, whether she wanted to be or not. She'd agreed to a few days. Now, without an income, she'd have to spend for ever with Luigi—or as long as it took for her to find another job and somewhere else to live! And the longer they stayed here the more settled Charlotte would become, and the harder it would be to move!

'I hate you, Luigi Costanzo.'

He smiled. 'You look beautiful when you're all fired up.'

At that moment Amy came in with a pot of freshly brewed tea, and the girl beamed when she heard Luigi tell Megan that she was beautiful. There was a skip to her step as she walked out.

'I think Amy approves of you,' he said, still with that aggravating smile.

'I don't care what she thinks,' Megan riposted. 'You had no right to do that. You're trying to make me your prisoner and I'm not.'

'Of course not, you're my wife,' he shot back at once. 'My very beautiful wife,' he added on a low growl. 'Red suits you; you should wear it more often. It makes your face come alive.'

'Flattery will get you nowhere,' she retorted coldly, her spine stiffening. She didn't want to be reminded of last night, when she had been uncomfortably aware of them both in their night clothes. It had brought back memories of the early weeks of their marriage when sometimes, at weekends, they hadn't bothered to get dressed at all.

Luigi used to say that he liked it when she was ready for him at any time, without the hindrance of top clothes with their buttons and zips and hooks. And she had to admit that she'd found it exciting too.

She poured herself a cup of tea, nibbled on a triangle of toast, and for once wished that he'd leave her and go to work. Contrarily, he showed no sign of moving. In fact, he gave the impression that he'd be happy sitting here all day.

'It's New Year's Eve tomorrow,' he reminded her.

Megan nodded. It was just another day as far as she was concerned. Another day in purgatory! Well, not quite, but that was how she preferred to think about it. She couldn't imagine living the rest of her life like this. If things were different between them, if he loved her, really loved her, and if he loved Charlotte the same way as she did, then perhaps there'd be hope. But not as things stood.

'I'm having a little get together.'

Megan frowned. 'You are?' She couldn't imagine Luigi celebrating New Year, not in his own home. Someone else's party, maybe, if it didn't interfere too much with his work. He'd probably network anyway. But a party here? There had to be some ulterior motive. 'Why?'

'It's time I brought this house alive. You've taught me that, Megan. Your reference to a mausoleum made me think. I'm going to open my doors to everyone I know.'

'Everyone? You said a little get together.'

'Perhaps not so little,' he agreed with a dangerous smile that revealed even white teeth.

He had beautiful teeth but they reminded her at that moment of the wolf in Little Red Riding Hood. Predatory! Here was the word again. 'So who are you inviting?'

'Business associates, colleagues, friends, neighbours. Anyone who cares to come.'

'And you didn't think to tell me?'

'I wanted it to be a surprise.'

'It's certainly that. Who's organising it?'

'Various people. Edwina and William are arranging everything here. Serena's seeing to the invitations—'

'Serena!' Megan slapped her toast down and glared at him. 'Why Serena? It should be my job.' She wished that she'd thrown the bread in his face; he deserved it. He was an out and out swine. Serena this, Serena that; she was always ingratiating herself into his favour. And how was she to know that he didn't share his PA's bed sometimes as well?

'Of course, my darling, but you know hardly anyone here yet. Next year you can write the list.'

'I doubt I'll be here next year,' she gritted through clenched teeth.

She wasn't looking at him but she heard his chair scrape back on the wooden floor and the next second he had hauled her to her feet and his big, strong hands were gripping her upper arms. 'You *will* be here,' he threatened. 'Haven't I made myself clear? I'm not letting you go again.'

'You won't be able to stop me,' she retorted. 'I won't have you flaunting Serena in my face. If you don't get rid of her, I go.'

Luigi's eyes narrowed damningly. 'You know I can't do that. She practically runs my business affairs for me.'

'That's no reason why she should run your private life as well. Unless she is part of that too! Is she?' She looked directly into his eyes and they didn't flicker.

'Megan, you are the only woman for me. You must believe that.'

She wanted to, but there were so many things that filled her with doubt and, just when she was beginning to learn to trust him, along came something else to threaten her tenuous hold. 'So you keep saying. I have little proof of it so far.'

His brows met, his eyes narrowed into dangerous slits. 'That's because you won't let me in.'

'With just cause. As you've this very second proved.'

'Serena is no threat to you.'

'She wants to be.'

'Maybe,' he admitted. 'But she's very well aware that you're now back in my life, a total part of it, and that there's no place for her. You have nothing to fear where she is concerned.'

'Really?' Megan doubted his conviction. And she noticed that he didn't say that Serena knew that he loved her. It was always missing. The one thing she most wanted to hear. *She was a total part of his life.* What the hell was that supposed to mean? Anyone could be a part of your life. Edwina the cook was a part of his life. As was Amy, and William, and now Kate.

'Truly. You'll see tomorrow. She'll probably be over early to oversee the final details. I—'

'No!'

Her sudden and savage exclamation brought his chin up with a jerk.

'I won't have that woman doing things that I should be doing. I'll see to everything—and I won't let you down,' she added caustically as she saw the beginnings of doubt creep across his face.

'You're jealous!' he accused with a swift smirk.

'Don't flatter yourself,' she tossed smartly. 'It's just that I don't think your business life and private one should intermingle. Serena can do what she likes in the office, but not here.'

He shrugged and his hands dropped from her shoulders. 'Very well, I'll leave it to you.'

'How many are you expecting?'

'About fifty.'

More than she'd thought. But there was a ballroom that would hold them all easily. She'd better go and see Edwina, check on the arrangements, see if there was anything she could do. 'Are you working today?' For once she wanted him out of the way.

'I thought I'd pop in for an hour or so.'

'Mummy, Mummy, we're having a party.' Charlotte charged into the room and threw herself at her mother.

Megan whirled her around and kissed her soundly. 'It's not for children, sweetheart.'

Her daughter's bottom lip began to drop.

'But if you're a very good girl, maybe Daddy and I will let you stay up for a little while. What do you say, Daddy?'

He lifted Charlotte into his arms, the first really natural gesture Megan had seen. 'For one hour, but that's all.'

'Are we having jelly and ice-cream?'

'It's not that sort of party, princess.'

Charlotte frowned. 'What sort then?'

'People drink and talk and dance, and at midnight everyone sings Auld Lang Syne and—'

'She won't understand any of that,' interrupted Megan. 'It's just a lot of grown ups, sweetheart, who do lots of boring things.'

'No children?'

'None at all.'

'I don't think I want to come then. Will you still read me a bedtime story, Mummy, or will you be too busy?'

'I'll never be too busy for you, my little darling.'

'And you, Daddy, will you read to me too?'

It was the first time she'd asked Luigi and Megan held her breath as she waited for his answer. She prayed he wouldn't reject her.

'Only if you tell me which story you want.'

'Yes, yes, the one about the little girl sliding down the rainbow.'

'Then I'll read it to you,' he said, 'but you'll have to help me because I'm not very good at reading to little girls.'

'Mummy's good at it. She'll help you.'

Megan smiled weakly. The thought of sitting side by side with Luigi reading to their daughter should have filled her with immense pleasure, but it didn't—because she knew he wouldn't have his heart and soul in it. He wasn't doing it because he wanted to, but because Charlotte had demanded it.

When Luigi finally left for the office Megan went in search of Edwina. William was already filling the ballroom with holly and mistletoe gathered from the estate, and Edwina was beside herself with excitement. 'It's been many a year since we had a party here, long before Mr Luigi took over. Oh, it's good to see the house being brought back to life again.'

Soon, Megan was immersing herself in the preparations. Even Charlotte helped, carefully watched over by a hovering Kate. Apparently Edwina had been baking and freezing for days and there was only the fresh food to be prepared as soon as it was delivered. The drinks arrived— enough cases of champagne and wine to last a lifetime, thought Megan, but she couldn't help getting caught up in the excitement of the occasion.

It was pandemonium at times, but with the gardener to help William, and both Amy and Megan helping Edwina, by the time Luigi came home all was ready. And there was even plenty of time for them to sit with Charlotte while she had a light tea. Afterwards Kate bathed her while Megan decided which of the dozen or so delectable dresses Luigi had given her for Christmas she was going to wear. Then they both sat at their daughter's bedside and took turns in reading to her until she fell asleep.

Megan was impressed by Luigi's rendition of The Rainbow Children. She had imagined a dull monologue; instead he'd put exactly the right inflection into his voice for each of the characters. She said as much to him.

'I imagined that if I'd ever had anyone read to me that's what I would have wanted.' There was a gruff grimness to his voice as he spoke, reminding her what an awful and loveless childhood he'd had. And it made her wonder whether she was being too hard on him.

But the moment they were out of Charlotte's room he spoilt it all by saying, 'Serena's going to be here early. She needs to check that—'

'Serena needs to check nothing,' Megan told him tersely. 'We've all worked like Trojans today and if there's something not quite right then it's too late to do anything about it. Phone and tell her.' She didn't want the other woman parading all over the place as though it was her rightful duty. Not while *she* was living in this house!

Megan took extra special care getting ready. She had a strong feeling that Serena would try to outdo her, that she would want to be the star of the evening. Of course, she might be wrong, but she couldn't forget the way the other woman had spoken to her. "I think Luigi will be available if you tell him who I am." "He's a fool not to have divorced her." If that didn't tell her that Serena had designs on him then nothing would.

She was glad now that Luigi had given her some beautiful dresses for Christmas. She'd decided on the red one, bearing in mind what he'd said about the colour suiting her. It was far more sophisticated and daring than anything she'd worn in the past, but as she slid the soft material over her head and smoothed the folds over her breasts and hips, she began to feel a different person. More elegant than ever before, full of confidence, totally in charge of her feelings. She could be whoever she wanted to be. And that person was Luigi's wife. In every respect!

Look out, Serena!

Their guests were arriving at eight. At a quarter to she was ready. Luigi tapped on her door and entered, and he took her breath away. His cream tuxedo and black trousers emphasised his fine physique and complemented his Latin colouring. She had never seen him so devastatingly handsome and crazily she wanted to rip off his clothes and make love to him.

'Megan, you look ravishing.'

Not half as ravishing as you, she thought, swallowing hard and moistening lips that had gone suddenly dry. In fact her whole mouth was dry. She needed a drink, a good stiff drink.

Luigi was looking at her as though he'd never seen her before, appraising every inch of her body, starting with the strappy, high-heeled silver sandals and her scarlet painted toenails. Over the long, softly flowing skirt which swirled about her ankles but clung lovingly to her slender hips, following it up to the deep vee which finished just below her breasts.

It was almost as though he was touching her. Wherever his eyes went she felt a burning sensation, and when he paused on the swell of her breasts she ached for him to touch her. It would have been so easy for him to cross the space that divided them and take what she was willing to give.

But he didn't move. He seemed transfixed. She wondered whether he had ever actually seen the dress before. Whether he had picked it personally or had his shop assistants pack half a dozen or so in her size. Probably so. But at this moment she didn't care.

It was doing things to both of them that should never be

allowed. She was thankful for the light support built into the dress that hid her peaking nipples. She didn't want anyone but Luigi to know how aroused she was. But she wanted him to know it; she needed him to want no one but her this evening.

The back of the dress dipped low as well, though he couldn't see that yet. He would find out when they danced together, when his hands held her close, when she felt the strong beat of his heart against her own. When they declared to the whole world that they were man and wife and no one could put them asunder. Lord, she was running ahead of herself. Was she ready for this yet? Was Luigi ready? Or was she doing it simply to spite Serena?

The dress was sleeveless and ruched on the shoulders, and beaded with intricate embroidery. This one dress alone must have cost him a small fortune. But she loved it.

'We'd better go down before I rip that thing off you and carry you to my bed,' he said gruffly.

Megan couldn't even speak. She simply nodded and smiled—weakly, and as she walked towards him her heart pounded like a sledge-hammer within her breast. 'Thank you for the dress, Luigi,' she said in a faint whisper.

'Thank you for wearing it. You look sensational. You'll knock everyone dead tonight, and I shall be so proud to introduce you as my wife.' He tucked her arm into his and together they walked along the landing and down the stairs.

Megan felt proud and she walked tall, and when the first person she set eyes on was Serena she grew another couple of inches.

At least she presumed it was Serena. Who else would be standing waiting at the bottom of the stairs? Their first guest to arrive, tall, slender and sophisticated with stunning flame-red hair and eyes only for Luigi.

Megan was able to study her and she didn't like what she saw. The woman was beautiful, and she knew it, and she had a poise that Megan had never possessed. Until she wore the red dress! It was a magic dress, as Charlotte would have said. It turned her into a different person.

Serena had green eyes, cat's eyes, which could spit fire if she so chose, and her dress was green too, a deep emerald taffeta, pinched in tight to emphasise her tiny waist, smooth over her stomach, but full at the back. And there was not an inch of bosom showing. It was a very clever dress. It moulded Serena's high, taut breasts to perfection. Tantalising but not revealing; making a man want to find out for himself what lay beneath.

Megan turned to see whether Luigi was as entranced as Serena obviously hoped he would be, and to her delight found that he was looking at her. He put his hand over hers where it lay on his arm and squeezed tightly. 'Serena,' he whispered below his breath.

'I guessed,' she replied in a husky voice.

'You have nothing to worry about.'

'I'm glad about that,' and she smiled lovingly into his face.

By this time they had reached his PA and Megan saw the swift coldness that entered her eyes.

'Megan, I'd like you to meet Serena, without whom my work would never flow freely. Serena, my wife.'

'The one who walked out of your life?' came the chilling response. Implying, thought Megan, that she had a nerve walking right back into it.

'The very same,' declared Megan cheerfully, 'but I'm here now—for good.' And she held out her hand.

The woman looked at her steadily for a few long seconds, as though trying to read her mind, wondering whether she was telling the truth, or whether it was all an act for her benefit. Truthfully, Megan wasn't sure either. They still had a lot of sorting out to do. And she couldn't help but wonder what Luigi had told her about his wife's return. Judging by Serena's careful scrutiny, Megan had a feeling he hadn't been entirely truthful.

But whatever, tonight Luigi was hers. Serena wasn't going to get a look in. Megan had never been the possessive type, but a woman had to draw the battle line somewhere.

Serena reluctantly shook her hand, but it was a very light, cool, impersonal touch, and she pulled quickly away. 'Luigi tells me that you've personally overseen arrangements here.' And she looked around her, as though hoping to find fault.

'Naturally,' answered Megan with forced exuberance. 'Come and look in the ballroom. I know you're going to love it.' In actual fact she knew nothing of the sort. It probably wasn't to Serena's taste, but there was no way she was going to give this other woman the opportunity to say so. 'And the food,' she continued, 'is perfect. Luigi has a treasure in Edwina. Between us we've provided a buffet that no one can fault.'

She very lightly touched Serena on the elbow and urged her in the direction of the ballroom. Over her shoulder she looked at Luigi and found him looking at her in stunned admiration. Round one to me, she thought.

And then the rest of the guests began to arrive, all of them curious to meet Luigi's wife. She was the centre of attention, much to Serena's chagrin. Megan saw her trying to be polite and friendly but constantly glancing in her and Luigi's direction. 'I think,' she said softly to her husband, 'that Serena's feeling her nose pushed out of joint.'

'Nonsense,' he declared, looking across at his assistant. 'Serena's in her element. She knows everyone here.'

He was so blind, thought Megan. Perhaps he *had* been speaking the truth when he said that there was nothing going on between them. But couldn't he see that the woman was in love with him? Weren't men's antennae alerted to that sort of thing? Didn't they take advantage? She wasn't sure that their relationship was purely the business one he would have her believe.

Luigi had hired a three-piece band and as the evening progressed Megan found herself whisked around the dance floor by several of Luigi's business colleagues and friends, all pumping her for information about their reconciliation. She was deliberately evasive. 'Delightfully so,' said one of her partners. 'I never even knew Luigi was married,' said another. 'Except to his work.' At which she was supposed to laugh. Unfortunately she didn't find it funny and gave a weak smile instead.

The buffet was an unmitigated success, although Serena only picked at it distastefully. Megan was talking to one of Luigi's business partners, keeping half an eye on what was going on around her, when she saw Serena dart over to her husband and take his arm. Luigi had only that second finished a conversation with someone else. Clearly the woman had been biding her time, had probably been doing so all evening. In fact Megan had made sure there was no opportunity for the two of them to get together, finding grim satisfaction in doing so.

Now she watched them closely and when she saw him lead Serena out of the room, his guiding hand lightly on her back, her heart felt as though it had turned to ice.

Megan wanted to follow but her companion of the moment was in the middle of what he clearly thought was an amusing story and she couldn't be rude enough to walk away. She watched the doorway, though, for their return, and long minute followed long minute. Ten minutes, twelve. Fifteen. What the hell were they doing?

Just as she knew that she could wait no longer they came back, Serena looking very smug, Luigi's eyes searching for hers. When he saw her he headed immediately in her direction, but Megan didn't want to speak to him, she didn't want to smell Serena's perfume on him, or see a smear of make-up on his collar, or lipstick on his cheek. She dashed smartly away, pretending not to have seen him, heading through one of the other doors and into a downstairs cloakroom.

A big mistake!

Serena followed.

CHAPTER NINE

MEGAN was checking her make-up in the mirror when the door opened and Serena entered, a confident smile playing about her lips and a light of triumph in her vivid green eyes. She looked like a cat who'd stolen the cream!

She sauntered over to Megan, but before she could say anything Megan blazed into attack. 'If you think that a five minute grope with my husband gives you any rights over him you're very much mistaken.' Immediately the words were out she regretted them. What had happened to her new-found poise? She oughtn't to have let Serena see that she was jealous.

Serena smiled, totally unperturbed. 'A five minute grope? I think I have slightly better taste than that. And so has Luigi, though perhaps you don't know him as well as you think. I bet he hasn't told you that he's still carrying on his affair with me. I don't mind being a kept woman. An illicit relationship is far more exciting, don't you think? Or perhaps you wouldn't know.'

Megan's stomach muscles clenched so tight that they hurt, as did her heart—it felt as though it had been crushed between two pieces of stone. 'Whatever you say, whatever Luigi promises you,' she retorted coldly. 'The truth is that

I am the one he comes home to at night. I am the one he loves. I am the one who has given him a daughter. And I shall never let him go again. Never!'

She had hesitated over the word *loves*. Luigi didn't love her; he loved no one—not even Serena. Or did he? Was this glamorous girl the reason he'd never proclaimed his love? She looked deep into Serena's eyes and saw the supreme confidence. This woman was so very, very sure of herself. Sure of Luigi's love! But Megan refused to give in to her fears. She faced Serena with her head held high, no doubt at all on her face that she was the one Luigi loved.

'I think perhaps you're underestimating Luigi,' said Serena, her voice low and sultry. 'He doesn't like to be stifled, he doesn't like to be held down by a child. He's a free spirit; he was happy in the years you were gone. *We* were happy. He's changed since you came back. You're a burden to him, Megan, I think you ought to know that.'

For a brief moment Megan closed her eyes. Despite all his denials, Luigi was still carrying on with Serena. He had never stopped. He was a liar and a cheat—and yet she still loved him. But enough to continue living with him? That was the question she had to ask herself.

'I'll leave you now to brew on those facts,' said Serena in a sugar-sweet voice. 'Perhaps they'll make you think twice about nesting with Luigi for, believe me, you're wasting your time; it will never last.'

Megan stood for several long moments after the red-haired girl had gone. Luigi had done a good job convincing her that there was nothing going on between him and his PA. And now Serena had made a mockery of every word he'd said. He was a liar and a cheat and she didn't know how she was going to get through the rest of the evening without telling him so.

* * *

Luigi looked everywhere for Megan. One minute she was in his sights, the next gone. It had annoyed him when Serena took him to one side with an urgent discussion about work, something that couldn't wait, she'd said. Which was nonsense. At one time he might have thought it important, but his home life was becoming his top priority these days. Unfortunately Serena couldn't seem to see it.

He supposed it was his own fault because he'd always been the one to keep her working late. When there was a job to be done he'd seen no sense in leaving it in the middle, working until midnight if necessary. And Serena had always co-operated. It was why he'd repaid her by taking her out for a meal now and then, and even a weekend away after they'd been particularly busy. But he wished she'd understand that things were changing now that Megan was back on the scene and he was a father.

A whole new direction had begun in his life, one he had never foreseen but he liked very much. Where *was* Megan? There was Serena looking very pleased with herself. She liked to think that she was the linchpin in all of his dealings, and she'd been a teeny bit peeved when Megan insisted that she wanted to handle the arrangements for tonight. But she'd been pleasant enough to Megan when they met so he didn't have any worries on that score.

Then he saw Megan, talking to a neighbour's wife at the other end of the room. He began to weave his way towards her. In truth he couldn't wait for the party to end. She looked so ravishing that he found it difficult to take his eyes off her. His whole system had gone into overdrive the second he'd seen her in that slinky red dress, and all he'd wanted to do was tear it off her and make furious love. That feeling hadn't diminished.

If it hadn't been their own party they could have sneaked

away for half an hour, but unfortunately they couldn't do that. He would have to be patient and wait, though the ache in his groin was almost unbearable. He couldn't remember ever wanting her as much as he did now, and the good part about it was that she wanted him too. He had seen it in her eyes.

'Megan, the dancing's started again.' He finally reached her and with a smile and an apology dragged her away from her companions. 'I can't wait for tonight to end,' he muttered in her ear as he held her close, his hand on the naked skin of her back. Lord, she felt so good, he thought, as they moved to the rhythm of the music, and he pressed her hard against him so that she could feel his raging desire.

He failed to notice that she wasn't looking at him quite so lovingly, or that her responses were fractionally cooler. It wasn't until the dance ended and she pulled away from him that he realised something had changed. 'Megan?' he asked with a frown. 'What's wrong?'

'Nothing.'

But it was too quick a response, and she hadn't quite met his eyes. 'Aren't you feeling well?'

'I'm all right,' she said quickly. Too quickly, he thought. Something was definitely going on in her mind. Was she regretting giving herself away earlier? Could that be it? If so he didn't care because he knew that once they were alone he would easily persuade her that she needed him as much as he needed her. He'd kept away for far too long.

He had thought he was doing the right thing, letting her come to him in her own time, but there was only so much a man could stand. And this abstinence was driving him crazy.

The music started up again, something slow and smoochy, and before she could move away he slid both arms around her and she had no option but to hold him too. He felt the faint, unsteady throb of her heart and he inhaled her sweet fragrance, but simply holding her was intoxicating his senses to such a degree that it was all he could do not to whisk her away up the stairs. 'You're the most beautiful woman in the room, did you know that?' he asked softly against her ear. 'Which makes me the luckiest man alive.'

She made some sort of response that he didn't quite catch, but which suggested that his compliment didn't altogether please her. And he couldn't understand why. 'Megan, are you sure there's nothing wrong?'

'Absolutely nothing,' she said, but he sensed it was false.

'I'm sorry if I haven't spent as much time with you as I'd have liked, but there are so many people who want to talk to me, and you, of course. You're quite the star of the evening. Everyone's telling me how beautiful you are, and how pleased they are that we're back together.'

'They have no idea,' she muttered, and he could feel acid dripping from her tongue.

Instantly he had dragged her away into the silence and privacy of another room. 'What's got into you, Megan?' he asked sharply, his fingers forcibly under her chin so that he could look into her eyes. Troubled eyes.

'Nothing,' she repeated stubbornly. 'And we oughtn't to shut ourselves away from our guests like this. They'll wonder what's going on.'

'*I* am wondering what's going on,' he retorted loudly. 'You can't suddenly change for no reason.'

'It's a woman's prerogative.'

'Rubbish! Someone's upset you. And, judging by the cold shoulder treatment, it would appear to be me. Am I right?'

Megan averted her eyes.

'Look at me, dammit.' He clenched her chin so tightly

that he knew it must hurt but she didn't even flinch. 'I said look at me.'

Slowly she did as he asked, and what he saw sent his heart crashing into his shoes. Hostility, hatred, accusation! Everything he had hoped never to see again. 'OK, what's going on?.'

'Need you ask?' Her grey eyes were filled with raw hurt and he wished he knew why.

'If I knew, I wouldn't be questioning you, would I?' Then something suddenly clicked in his brain. 'It's Serena, isn't it?' And he laughed with relief. 'You saw us leave the ballroom? My dearest Megan, that was pure business. Serena lives and breathes it, the same as I used to. I tried to tell her it wasn't important, that it would wait until we were back in the office, but no, she needed to talk it over with me.'

'And that's all there was to it?' She looked as though she didn't believe him.

'I swear it.'

'If you say so.' But it was clear she didn't accept that he was telling the truth. 'Dammit, Megan, where has all this come from? I could have sworn earlier that you were as ready for me as I was for you. And now it's all gone.'

'And you can't guess why? But for your sake I'll behave exactly how you want me to—until our guests leave.'

And then she would shut him out! He let his breath whistle through his teeth. He would never understand her, not in a million years. She had nothing to fear where Serena was concerned; how was he going to convince her of that?

Suddenly the door was pushed open and the woman who was the cause of their dissension poked her head inside. 'Ah, there you are.' At a glance she took in the fierce glare on Megan's face and Luigi's unhappiness, and her smile was wide.

'I wondered where you two lovebirds had got to. It's almost midnight; we need to charge our glasses. Coming, Luigi?'

Luigi looked at Megan and saw the green sparks of jealousy shooting from her eyes. 'We'll be out in a minute,' he told Serena. Part of him was glad that Megan was so deeply jealous, but the other half knew that it was not going to be easy winning her round.

What they needed to do was sit down and talk, get everything out into the open, lay all their cards on the table. Perhaps, with the start of a new year, they could do that. A new year, a new relationship. He couldn't go on like this, that was for sure. After their guests had gone he would insist that they have a heart to heart. For now he would have to accept that she was simply play-acting.

When Serena closed the door he took Megan's hands and their eyes met. She looked so miserably unhappy that he wanted to kiss her and promise that everything would be all right. But when he arched his head towards her she drew away.

'Let's get it over with,' she said abruptly.

And for the rest of the night she was the life and soul of the party, throwing herself wholeheartedly into singing 'Auld Lang Syne', singing the loudest, laughing the longest. She was too happy, brittly so, but no one knew it except himself.

And, of course, Serena, but he was unaware of that.

Megan didn't know how she managed to act as though nothing was wrong; it was hard when your heart was broken in two and you knew that it could never be repaired. Luigi was an out and out liar. Did he really think that she didn't know what he'd been up to? She had known, even without Serena telling her, but to have it confirmed so blatantly, so cheerfully, had frozen every vein and nerve inside her. Nor had she been able to hide her hurt from Luigi, no matter how much she'd wanted to. In fact she couldn't remember anything about the latter part of the evening. Except Serena's gloating smile every time their eyes met.

She had shaken hands and made the right platitudes, but when everyone had gone, when she and Luigi were alone at last, she stripped the façade away. She looked at him with hatred in her eyes. 'What a fiasco. I'm glad it's over. I'm going to bed, goodnight.'

But Luigi was having none of it. 'We're going to talk. *Now!*'

'It won't do any good,' she said bitterly. Was he blind or stupid or both? She'd felt happier today than she had in a long time—until Serena stuck the knife in. It still hurt, and it proved that her husband was a consummate liar, and why he never professed any love for her 'First thing in the morning I'm packing my bags.'

Luigi looked as though he'd been turned to stone. He didn't speak; he simply stood there looking at her, total incredulity in his eyes.

'I've given it a good try,' she added. 'We've had a good Christmas and New Year, and I thank you for that. Now it's time for me to go back to my old life—where I was happy and contented. And you'll be able to carry on as many love affairs as you like.'

Megan found that she was breathing hard by the time she'd finished. She couldn't look at Luigi now without seeing Serena at his side—a smiling, complacent Serena, confident in the knowledge that Luigi preferred her to his wife. There was a red blur in front of her eyes, red rage that matched the colour of her dress. Luigi became the devil with horns. The red turned to black—to nothing.

Megan was unaware that Luigi caught her in his arms as she began to fall to the floor in a dead faint.

When she came to, Megan was being carried up the stairs, Luigi's strong arms around her. She felt fear and alarm and began to struggle, unable to comprehend what was going on. How had she ended up here?

'Keep still!' he warned. 'You fainted. I'm taking you to your room. You need to lie down.'

She closed her eyes; she didn't want to see the look of love and tenderness on his face. It had never been there before. Why now? Was it a trick of the light? 'Fainted?' she echoed. 'I've never fainted in my life. If this is some ploy to—'

'It's nothing of the kind,' he assured her, the softness disappearing, making her realise that she must have imagined it. 'I think the evening proved too much for you. You were on your feet all day, and then…'

Megan stopped listening. She was remembering the real reason for her distress, and she began to struggle even more violently.

'Dammit, keep still,' warned Luigi, his arms tightening around her. 'Are you trying to get us both killed?'

They reached the top of the stairs, but he still didn't put her down, despite her continuing fight. He waited until he had kicked open the door and carried her across to her bed before he finally released her.

Megan immediately sprang up again, but was unprepared for the dizziness that overcame her, and was compelled to sit back down, a hand to her forehead and a dazed look in her eyes.

Luigi fetched her a glass of water. 'Sip that slowly until you feel better,' he commanded.

Suddenly subdued, Megan did as he asked. She had clearly worked herself up to such a pitch that everything had exploded inside her head. What she needed to do now was be calmly organised. She still intended to leave, but she would do it quietly one day while Luigi was at work. She wouldn't go back to the house she had shared with Jenny, but would find somewhere else where her husband would never find her.

'Are you feeling better?' To give him his due, Luigi looked genuinely concerned. It would be so easy to believe that she was the only woman in his life—if the image of a pair of gloating green eyes didn't continually haunt her!

She nodded. 'I'll be all right now.' Meaning, please leave. But he didn't take the hint.

'Let me help you get undressed and into bed.'

There was such tenderness and concern in his voice that it almost broke her in two. But she knew it was an act. He wanted the best of both worlds. A wife and daughter, *and a mistress on the side!* She sat bolt upright, slamming the glass down on the bedside table.

'I wouldn't let you help me if you were the last man on earth,' she yelled. 'Get out! *Get out now!*' So much for her plans to lull him into a false sense of security and then quietly disappear. How could she live for even a minute longer with a two-timing swine like him?

'If this is still about Serena—'

'You can bet it's about Serena,' she tore in furiously. 'You're welcome to her, and she to you.'

'But—'

'But nothing,' she thrust, pushing herself up from the bed and hastening across the room to open the door so that he could leave.

He made no attempt to move, simply following her with his eyes, sad eyes, she noticed. What a good actor he was. 'Serena means nothing to me.'

'So you keep saying.'

'It's the truth.'

She lifted her shoulders.

'But you don't believe me?'

'No.'

'Why? You have no proof that anything's going on. It's all in your suspicious little mind.' He took a step forward.

Megan froze. 'Maybe I do have proof, not that I intend to share it with you.'

Luigi frowned. 'How can there be proof when—'

'When you don't feel anything for her? Spare me the platitudes, Luigi. Just get the hell out of here.'

His lips thinned to a narrow, straight line and to her relief he marched determinedly towards the door. But when he reached it he came to an abrupt halt and turned to face her, his eyes mere inches away from hers. Megan's breathing quickened. Despite everything he could still melt her bones, still send her crazily into a state of readiness. Such was his power! It looked as though she was destined to love him for the rest of her life.

Which made her even angrier.

'I realise there's no point in me saying anything more tonight,' he said grimly, his eyes steely hard. 'Not while you're in this mood. Your over-active little mind is putting two and two together and making five. But I'll prove to you that you're wrong. Tomorrow I'll fetch Serena here and she can tell you herself that you're worrying for nothing.'

He didn't wait for her response. He swung away and she slammed the door behind him. Too late she thought of Charlotte and Kate, and prayed that she hadn't woken them.

What good would it do, Serena coming here? The woman would lie through her teeth, not for one nanosecond wanting Luigi to hear of the conversation she'd had with his wife.

Maybe she ought to pack now and disappear before he woke up in the morning. Unfortunately it was New Year's Day. Not an ideal time to find alternative accommodation.

She threw herself down on the bed and punched her frustration out on the pillow. Damn Luigi! Damn Serena! And she was still damning them to eternal hell when sleep overtook her.

Two hours later she woke, shivering. With desperate fingers she ripped off her dress, uncaring whether she tore it in the process, then pulled on her nightdress and curled up beneath the softly padded quilt. But sleep was far away now. Anger and hatred filled the rest of her night.

Daylight was beginning to steal through the sky when she finally dropped off and she dreamt that the green-eyed Serena, in her hateful green dress, was floating above her, a leering glitter in her eyes. And she was pleading with Serena to let her share Luigi. Serena laughed, a mocking laugh that echoed in Megan's ears as she awoke.

Charlotte and Kate were in Charlotte's room and her daughter was laughing helplessly. Megan climbed out of bed and opened the dividing door.

'I'm sorry if we woke you,' apologised Kate at once.

'It's all right,' said Megan as Charlotte hurled herself into her mother's arms. She held her daughter close, immediately expunging the bad memories. 'What were you laughing at, sweetheart?'

'Nanny was tickling me. Was it a good party, Mummy? I wanted to come down but Nanny said I mustn't because it was only for grown-ups.'

'That's right, and actually, my darling, it was a bit boring. I didn't know anyone except your daddy and Serena.'

'Who's Serena?'

'She works for Daddy.'

'Is she pretty?'

'Very pretty.'

'That's good, 'cos Daddy likes pretty things. He told me so. He told me I was pretty, and that he loved you 'cos you were pretty as well.'

Megan's veins stiffened as an electric shock ran through them. Luigi had said that? But the feeling quickly faded as she accepted that Luigi's declaration of love would have been a throwaway comment, something to please a little girl anxious for affection. The aftermath left her feeling more dispirited than ever.

'Will you come and have your breakfast with us?' asked Charlotte eagerly. She had been encouraged into the routine of eating her meals with her nanny in the newly furnished nursery.

'Of course I will, my precious.' Anything to avoid seeing Luigi.

She wondered whether he was still serious about fetching Serena. Maybe he would have realised after sleeping on it that it would do no good. But probably not! When Luigi had a bee in his bonnet he stuck with it. He was adamant about wanting to prove that Serena had no part to play in his private life. Of course he would prime the woman first; that would be his reason for picking her up. He wouldn't just phone and say, 'Come over.' They needed to consolidate their strategy.

She and Kate were laughing over something Charlotte had said when Luigi walked into the nursery. His frown was deep when he saw her. 'Why are you here?' he asked, and she could see that he was trying desperately, for his daughter's sake, not to sound cross.

'Charlotte invited me.'

'And it didn't matter that I was sitting downstairs waiting for you?'

Megan became aware of Kate's raised eyebrows. 'I'm sorry, I should have told you,' she said in a deliberately warm voice. 'Why don't you join us? I'll ask Amy to send—'

'I've already eaten,' he announced abruptly, 'but I'd appreciate it if you'd find time to join me for coffee.' And with that he turned abruptly on his heel and left.

'Oops!' said Kate.

'It's all right,' returned Megan, smiling. 'I'd forgotten there was something he wanted to talk about.'

'Then you should go now, not keep him waiting any longer.'

And, although Kate tried to pretend that everything was perfectly normal, Megan could see that she was besieged with curiosity.

Ten minutes went by before she finally joined Luigi. Ten minutes in which he'd had time to grow even angrier. 'Were you deliberately avoiding me?' he rasped.

'Actually, yes,' she answered calmly. 'I didn't like the tone of our conversation last night. I had no wish to carry it on.'

'Ah, you didn't like the tone.' His voice was heavily condescending. 'And how do you think I felt when I was accused of doing something that I'm not guilty of?'

'So you say,' she retorted smartly.

'I am not a liar,' he slung back.

'And I'm not in the habit of making things up.'

'You see what you want to see.'

'I hear what I don't want to hear,' she thrust.

'And what is that supposed to mean?' The frown was harsh again, slicing his brow in two, eyes as hard as metal bullets.

'You work it out.'

'I'm aware,' he said slowly, 'that there's gossip about Serena and myself. Ugly rumours. It's natural in a workplace. So who's been speaking out of turn? Tell me and I'll damn well sack them.'

Megan found it hard to believe that he was still doing his utmost to deny a relationship with his good-looking PA. If his business colleagues were talking about it then it must be true. The maxim that there was no smoke without fire was almost always spot on.

'I have no wish to divulge my source of information,' she told him icily. 'I expect it will come out in time. These things always do. Meanwhile I don't wish to speak with Serena, or even see her again. I wouldn't believe her if she swore on the Bible.' Her heart was banging away in her chest like a kid bouncing a ball on the pavement. Thump, thump, thump. Thump, thump, thump. And everywhere else her body tingled and pulsed and resented every inch of this man standing in front of her.

He was wearing a black sweater this morning and black trousers and, added to his swarthy skin and raven-black hair, menace leaked from every pore in his body. At one time, when he dressed in black, she had thought it was sexy, turning her on like never before, but not this morning. In her eyes he was the devil incarnate.

Luigi's nostrils dilated as he strove for self-control. Something had gone radically wrong last night. Someone had said something out of school and Megan had believed them. The jealousy that he'd seen, and been pleased about, had turned into something ugly and dangerous and his whole future lay in the balance.

She had threatened to walk out on him again. Would she? His heart had stopped when she hadn't appeared at the breakfast table. He had feared the worst, racing up to her room to check on her wardrobe, his relief knowing no bounds when he'd discovered that her clothes were still there. Or were they simply the ones he had bought her? Another mind-stopping moment as he rifled through her drawers. Nothing had gone. He had checked Charlotte's room next, to make sure. He was safe. His daughter's clothes hung in the wardrobe.

He had been both relieved and angry when he'd found Megan in the nursery. There was no doubt in his mind that she was avoiding him and it had been hard for him not to drag her away. And now she stood before him as prickly as a hedgehog sensing danger, believing he was having an affair with Serena!

'How can I prove to you that you're wrong?' he asked, his arms spread wide, his palms open and towards her. His whole body was rigid, and he knew there was exasperation in his eyes; he couldn't help it. She was driving him insane.

'By sacking Serena. Banishing her from your life altogether.'

He stared at her with a mixture of horror and anger. 'I can't do that. She knows the business inside out. I'd be lost without her.'

'And would she be lost without you?' came Megan's caustic response.

She wasn't talking about work either. If only he knew who had put these suspicions into her mind he would have him hung, drawn and quartered without mercy. Or at the very least he would have him retract his statement in front of Megan. There was a very real danger here of him losing both his wife and his child because someone had stupidly repeated unfounded rumours.

No, not his child—he would *never* let Charlotte go. She was his flesh and blood. If all else failed and he couldn't persuade Megan to stay, then he would fight tooth and nail for custody of their daughter. She had added a very real meaning to his life, and he would never treat her the way he had been treated as a boy.

'You're seeing things that aren't there,' he said sharply. 'You shouldn't listen to gossip. But I'm not going to beg and ask to be given a chance to prove it. A woman of your integrity should know fact from fiction.' Lord, she was spectacularly beautiful this morning. Why was it that a woman aroused, whether in anger or in lust, always looked beautiful, whereas an angry man looked ugly?

'Last night you threatened to leave me. Are you still of that mind?'

She hesitated a moment before nodding.

His lips thinned. 'We seem to have had this conversation before,' he told her drily and not a little impatiently. 'But perhaps I'd better reiterate one point. Charlotte stays.'

Megan's chin jerked and her eyes hardened. 'We came as a package, Charlotte and I, and that's how we'll leave.'

'Then you'd better think very hard about your decision. Because, believe me, wherever you go I'll find you.'

In answer Megan swung on her heel and walked away, leaving him with no idea what she intended to do.

CHAPTER TEN

MEGAN spent the whole morning considering her future. She had no doubt that Luigi meant every word. He *would* find them. No place would be safe. And he would take away his daughter. She would be left with an empty life. Merely the thought of Serena being a mother to Charlotte sent cold nervous shivers down her spine.

Serena thought of no one but herself; she would resent having a sometimes recalcitrant child under her feet. She would probably send her away to boarding school as soon as she was old enough and Charlotte would hate that. And so would Megan. Over her dead body would she allow him to take Charlotte away from her!

On the other hand, she couldn't stay here and ignore Luigi's affair. She had hoped desperately that he'd learn to love her as she loved him. She'd been jealous of Serena, yes, but had prayed that the woman meant nothing to her husband. She had tried so hard to believe him. To what avail?

It was lunchtime before she saw Luigi again. She'd heard him go out, and no prize money for guessing where he'd gone, but she hadn't realised that he was back. Amy had laid the table, coming to find her to tell her that lunch was ready. Rather than upset her by declaring that she'd share with Kate and Charlotte again, Megan had made her way into the dining room, coming to a sudden halt when she saw Luigi sitting there.

He smiled as though nothing was wrong. He had changed out of his black gear and instead wore a blue polo shirt and grey slacks. He looked far more relaxed than he had earlier, no doubt due to Serena's influence, thought Megan caustically. She slid into the chair opposite him.

'No work today?' she asked, in an attempt to make conversation.

He shook his head. 'New Year's Day's an official holiday.'

'And one you don't usually adhere to.'

'I'm reformed, or are you forgetting?' he asked with a winning smile.

Megan was confused. He was acting as though nothing had happened. Was this going to be his strategy? Was he hoping that he could win her round by ignoring their argument? Not a cat in hell's chance! But as she didn't want her daughter seeing them at loggerheads she'd go along with it for now.

There had been a further sprinkling of snow during the night and after lunch the four of them went outside to play snowballs. Charlotte was in her element, and Kate almost as bad. They had a riotous time—until Charlotte wandered too far away from the house in search of deeper snow.

Megan wasn't concerned, and she didn't give the lake a thought until Luigi gave a yell and raced frantically towards it. Fear gripped her then with icy fingers and she chased after him. 'Charlotte!' she screamed. *'Charlotte!'* How could she have fallen in with three adults to watch over her? What had they been doing? Snowballing each other, that was what, like big kids let out of school.

Luigi stripped off his jacket and shoes and jumped in

and Megan's heart was in panic mode. She should have kept a closer eye on her daughter. The lake was deep in the centre but not around the edges, but even a few inches was enough for Charlotte to drown.

She could see her now, lying in the water, and big, wet tears mixed with her terror. 'Oh, my God, my baby!' She began to tear off her own jacket, her throat tight with fear, but Luigi had reached her and pulled a painfully still Charlotte up into his arms.

Megan thought she was dead—she was so white and still—but Luigi gave her a thump on the back and she coughed and spluttered and spilled out the water she'd swallowed. After that she started crying and asking for her mummy.

'I'll carry her into the house,' said Luigi roughly.

Megan ran at his side, constantly reassuring her daughter that everything was going to be all right. Charlotte was blue around the lips and shivering violently.

'I'll run a warm bath,' said Kate, who was as pale and shocked as the rest of them.

'Should we send for the doctor?' asked Luigi.

'Not unless she goes into a state of shock,' declared Kate, and they were both reassured by her confidence.

Megan stripped her daughter and gently helped her into the warm bath water, comforting her all the time, and gradually her colour returned to normal and she stopped crying and gave a weak smile.

Luigi had stood in the background watching. Now Megan turned to him and saw that he was shivering too. 'You fool,' she said. 'Go and take a hot shower or it'll be you we take to hospital.'

'Is she going to be all right?' There was a tremor in his voice and tears glistened in his eyes.

'I think so.'

'That damn lake; I'll get it filled in. Charlotte could so easily have drowned.'

'No, she couldn't,' assured Megan. 'We were all there, keeping our eye on her.'

'We didn't see her go in that direction. And one day she might be outside alone. I can't take the risk. I never thought. Oh, Megan, what if—'

She didn't wait to hear the rest. Instead, she wrapped her arms around him, wet as he was, and said, 'No what if's. She's all right, thanks to you. It's a beautiful lake, you can't do that.'

'Then I'll fence it. No parent should have to go through this.'

And Megan agreed with him.

It moved her, seeing him so upset. It proved how much he'd come to love his daughter. Even if he was unable to express himself openly, the feelings were there.

Charlotte appeared to suffer no ill effects from her dip in the icy water but for the rest of the day she wanted her mummy and daddy rather than Kate. Megan watched Luigi as he played with her, throwing himself whole-heartedly into whatever game she suggested. And he gave her spontaneous hugs and whispered words in her ear that Megan wasn't supposed to hear. But it sounded suspiciously as though he was telling her that he loved her.

It brought a lump to Megan's throat to see this man, whose business life had always meant so much more to him than anything else in the world, baring his soul to his daughter. It proved miracles did happen. And, even if he didn't love her, it meant a lot that he loved Charlotte. Once again she wondered whether it would be fair to take Charlotte away from him.

Simply looking at them together she could see the adoration in Charlotte's eyes. He was the epitome of all she'd ever wanted in a father. She had asked Santa Claus for him and he had provided the goods. Their daughter would be devastated if he was taken from her now. On the other hand, how could she live with a man who was carrying on an affair with another woman? She was in a catch-22 situation and there seemed to be no way out.

When it was bedtime Charlotte insisted that Luigi carry her up and tuck her in. Whether it was because he was the one who had rescued her, or because he'd given her more attention than ever before, Megan couldn't be sure, but whatever, she didn't want to let her father go.

He read her two stories before she fell asleep, her tiny hand clutched in his big one. Afterwards Luigi took Megan's hand and led her from the room. 'Let's go and sit in the den before dinner.' And in her mellowed mood Megan didn't demur.

The first thing he did was apologise again for what had happened.

'It's not your fault,' she assured him, 'though I have to admit I have had faint reservations about the lake.'

'You should have said,' he returned at once. 'I'd have done something about it.'

'If our situation had become permanent I would have.'

A shadow darkened his brow. 'I don't want you to leave, Megan. You and Charlotte mean so much to me.'

Her eyebrows lifted. '*I* do?'

'You're my wife. What do you think?'

Yes, that was right. She was his wife. And it was his duty to care about her. *But he didn't!* Or he wouldn't be carrying on with another woman. Not wanting to start another argument, she let it pass. Instead she said, 'I hope Charlotte doesn't suffer any after effects.'

'Is there a chance?' he asked with an instant frown. 'Should we have taken her to hospital?'

'I don't think so. We just need to keep an eye on her.'

'I'll sit with her all night if necessary.'

'There's no need for that,' she said gently. 'I'll hear her if she wakes.'

'You didn't hear her the other day,' reminded Luigi.

'Tonight I'll be listening.'

'We could listen together.'

Megan's whole sensory system stirred into life. Sitting here with him, a cosy log fire burning in the grate, the rich red curtains drawn against the cold winter's night, it was easy to forget everything else and remember only the good times they'd had. Amazingly, despite all that she'd gone through, she found herself still wanting him.

And, judging by the intensity in his eyes, he wanted her too.

Take what's on offer, she told herself. Easier said than done. How could she let him make love to her when the image of gloating green eyes would hover and disturb? Lord, she wanted him, but, hell, she couldn't have him! No, that was wrong. She *could* have him, but not on her own terms. Terms which would exclude Serena from his life for evermore.

'Megan.' His voice was soft and persuasive. 'I want this thing to work. I want you and Charlotte with me for all time.'

'I know,' she said on a husky whisper. 'But I can't—'

'Forget what you've heard?' he interjected with a slight edge to his voice. 'I wish I knew who had told you. It's lies, you know. All lies.'

'Can you prove that to me?'

'Only if you let Serena tell you herself.'

'No!' Megan shook her head quickly. 'The proof has to come from you.'

'You mean I have to cut her out of my life completely?' And when she gave a faint nod, 'I can't do that. It's impossible.'

She refused to break eye contact, hard though it was to see him struggling with his conscience. 'Then there's no future for us.'

Neither of them had raised their voices. It was a calm, civilised conversation and Megan congratulated herself on controlling her temper. Yelling at each other had got them nowhere.

'I happen to think that there could be,' he said, 'and for that reason I'm taking you away for a few days.'

Megan felt an instant surge of outrage. Not this again. It would be a pointless and futile exercise.

But before she could speak he went on swiftly, 'Not Charlotte; she's staying with Kate. Just you and me and I won't take no for an answer. More than ever we need this time to sort ourselves out. We're leaving straight after breakfast in the morning—providing Charlotte's OK, of course.'

'You can't do this,' she protested. 'It won't work. Nothing will.'

'I beg to differ.' His dark eyes were steady on hers, daring her to refuse him. 'It's what I've been trying to do ever since you came here. And I sorely wish now that we'd done it before your mind was poisoned.'

'As far as I can see,' she said, averting her gaze because he was causing another agonising dance of prickles over her skin, 'it wouldn't have made any difference. The truth would have come out in the end.'

'Yes, the truth!' he said with an edge of irony to his tone. 'I can assure you it *will* manifest itself. As you say, it always does. And on that day you and I will renew our wedding vows.'

He sounded so confident that Megan wanted to laugh. He was living a dream. There was no future between them, except as Charlotte's parents. For their daughter's sake they might keep up a pretence of normality—she was wavering as always, wondering whether she should leave or not, hating herself for being so weak-willed—but he would have Serena to satisfy his hormonal urges, while she would have no-one. Her life would be barren and empty and filled with pain. She wished with all her heart that she'd never gone into Gerards on that particular day.

'So where are you thinking of taking me?' Arguing seemed pointless. He would have his way no matter what so she might as well go along with his decision. Not that she could see any good coming out of it. And if he thought he was going to get her into bed then he would be sorely disappointed.

'That would be telling,' he said. 'But I know you'll approve.'

Luigi felt excitement such as he hadn't experienced in a long time. It had been easier than he'd expected persuading Megan to join him and now that she'd agreed he found his mind running on ahead. He would use the time to convince her that he wasn't the villain of the piece. He would use every skill he possessed to make her forget Serena and accept that he was the love of her life—as she was of his!

The fact that someone had thoughtlessly ruined what fragile hold they'd had on their relationship filled him with despair every time he thought about it. And one day he would get to the bottom of it, of that he was sure. But for the moment he was determined to concentrate on the days that lay ahead. He'd thought hard and long where to take her and had found the perfect place.

When morning dawned and Charlotte was her usual bright and cheerful self he breathed a sigh of relief. There was nothing now to stop them—except Megan. Half expecting her to have had a change of heart and prepared to use his powers of persuasion all over again, he was pleasantly surprised at breakfast when she confessed that she was all packed and ready. She didn't look happy about it but for the moment he didn't care.

He loaded the car and straight after breakfast they left, Charlotte waving them off a little tearfully, but accepting that they'd be gone only a few days and that Kate would be there to look after her.

After a few minutes travelling in silence he looked across at her. 'Don't look so miserable, Megan. It's not the end of the world.'

'I've never left Charlotte before.'

It wasn't the answer he'd expected so he grinned warmly. 'I'm sure she'll survive. She loves Kate. They'll have a whale of a time together.'

'What if she resents me when I get back? What if she loves Kate more than me?'

'How can she do that?' There was warm reassurance in his eyes. 'You're everything to her. She'll be counting the days. I saw her and Kate making a calendar this morning.'

She looked better after that and began to take an interest in the scenery around her. It was unusual for them to have snow this far south during the Christmas and New Year period. Everything had a picture-book quality and she was as excited as her daughter would have been as they rounded each bend and saw something different. It enchanted him just looking at her.

'It seems a shame to be leaving all this behind,' she said.

'Who said anything about leaving it behind?'

Megan frowned. 'I assumed we were going abroad. A few days in the sun. I've brought my passport.'

'Why waste time on a plane? As I said before, Megan, you're going to love this place. Now, don't ask any more questions. Sit back and enjoy the drive.'

They travelled north on the motorway. There were parts of the landscape with no snow at all. Others had deep pockets where in the distance Megan could see children tobogganing and making the most of this early fall of snow. She began to relax, though she couldn't help thinking about Charlotte and how much she was missing her already.

They stopped for lunch at a motorway service area but they didn't linger as Luigi was anxious to push on. Megan began to relax. Their conversation was desultory, Luigi making no demands other than she enjoy herself. And she did her best to forget about Serena and her influence over him, concentrating on the present instead. It wasn't difficult, not with her dark Latin husband at her side, oozing sexuality from every pore.

She had no idea what lay ahead, what trials or tribulations, what pleasures or delights. She was going to take each day as it came.

Maybe—a thought suddenly struck her, a glaringly simple idea that should have occurred to her before. If she relented and slept with him, if she let him share both her bed and her body, and she freed every one of her inhibitions, he would forget about Serena. They'd always had a superb sex life, and had proved at Christmas that nothing had changed. It could even be better!

Would that be the answer?

Would it be her weapon against this other woman?

If she gave Luigi everything he wanted he would have no need to look elsewhere!

Lord, she'd been blind!

The answer to all her problems was staring her right in the face. Only one thing was missing. His declaration of love! But why let that worry her? It hadn't in the past. It was just a word. It was feelings that counted, feelings and emotions and a sense of *being* loved. Luigi could say as many times as he liked that he loved her, but it meant nothing unless he showed it in every little way possible. And already he'd begun to do that by taking more time off from his business affairs.

Suddenly she felt happier than she had in a long time.

'Why are you grinning?'

Megan hadn't realised that her devious strategy was showing and she turned to look at her husband. 'Was I?' As if she didn't know!

'You look beautiful.'

It was going to be so easy! Already her hormones were racing, vying for position, ready to act on her every whim.

Were they going to Scotland? she wondered, as he drove further and further north. It would be fantastic at this time of year, especially if they'd had snow too. But a little before then, as they reached Cumbria and the Lake District, he left the motorway.

'The Lakes!' she exclaimed, her excitement showing. 'I've always wanted to go.' So many people had told her how beautiful the area was, with its mountains and lakes. It was where William Wordsworth had lived, and Beatrix Potter, and she'd always promised herself to come but had never made it.

'You look like Charlotte,' he said, 'when she first saw the snow.'

'I probably feel like her.' Megan couldn't hide her pleasure—not that it was all connected with where they were going! Her devious plan whirled round and round in her mind. If all went well she would get her husband back again—a reformed man who spent more time with his wife and child—and Serena would be left out in the cold. His PA might even decide that she could no longer work for him.

Megan wanted to throw her arms up into the air and whoop—except that explanations would be required! So she contented herself with a further inane grin.

It was dark when they reached their destination. They passed through a gateway guarded by tall iron gates into the grounds of a big house, lit up by floodlights that made it look like Buckingham Palace. For a moment Megan was disappointed. From one mansion without a heart to another!

But before she could say anything, Luigi veered off the main path and drove down a much narrower one overhung with the bare branches of trees. It ran for perhaps a third of a mile before their headlights picked out the shape of a log cabin huddling in the shadow of giant firs.

'We're staying here?'

He nodded. 'It belongs to a friend of mine who's in the Bahamas at the moment.'

'But he knows we're using it?'

'Of course.'

Megan got out of the car and ran over to the cabin. She could see smoke curling from the chimney and a light inside and she turned questioningly to Luigi, who was close on her heels.

'I gave instructions for it to be got ready. Open the door; it's not locked.'

Cautiously Megan did as he asked. Warmth greeted them. She stepped over the threshold. What a fantastic place! The central fireplace spilled its heat into the huge living area. There was plenty of comfortable seating and a dining table and chairs in one corner.

She explored further. One door led into a rustic kitchen, where a delicious smell of cooking assailed her nostrils, making her realise how hungry she was. Before she could ask questions, Luigi opened another door that led into a bathroom, and the third into a bedroom with two single beds. Mmm, that might prove difficult. Unless they shared, of course! Very cosy, but comfortable? Doubtful!

Then she spotted an open staircase going up from one corner and, catching Luigi's eye, he nodded, as if to say, Go on, go and have a look up there. At the top was a galleried landing overlooking the living area beneath, but, set back out of sight from anyone downstairs, was a huge bed covered in a magnificent red and gold woven quilt. Chunky wooden furniture accompanied it and through a stable type door, with the top half missing—her brows lifted at this—was a shower room. Not a bog-standard one, a huge one. You could hold a party in the shower basin, she thought, as her eyes roved over shelves filled with towels and toiletries. There was no window and the lighting was cleverly concealed. The whole effect, of both the bathroom and the bedroom, was stunningly erotic. There was no other word for it.

'You like?' asked Luigi.

Megan hadn't realised that he was standing quite so close behind her. 'It's—er—different,' she agreed. It was too soon yet to begin her plan of action. Actually it was perfect. It was planned for seduction. Was this what Luigi had in mind too? For some reason she hadn't thought along those lines; she'd been so excited by her own vivid thoughts. But perhaps he had known what to expect. Perhaps he'd been here before. With Serena!

The thought made her feel violently sick.

'What's the matter?' asked Luigi at once, seeing the sudden change in her.

'Nothing.'

'Nothing, my foot. Are you not feeling well? Or are you hungry? You only pecked at your food at lunchtime. What was I thinking? Come, let's go and eat. I'll unload the car later.'

Downstairs, he insisted that she sit while he laid the table. He opened a bottle of wine, cut thick chunks of fresh crusty bread, and sat the steaming casserole dish in the centre. 'Let's get started,' he said. 'I'm ravenous too if the truth's known.'

By this time Megan had pulled herself together. Did it matter whether Serena had been here or not? She was fighting for her marriage. This was her best chance at expurgating the other woman from his mind and, hopefully, his life. And she had to grab it with both hands.

'Who did this?' she asked, indicating the excellent beef Stroganoff.

'Michael's housekeeper.'

'And Michael is?'

'My friend who owns the big house. We met through business.'

'We must thank his housekeeper; this is wonderful.'

'*If* we see her,' he said with a wry lift of an eyebrow. 'She's stocked the cupboards and freezer with enough food to last a fortnight.'

'Who did you tell your friend was accompanying you?'

He pretended to look shocked. 'Why, my wife, of course. Michael thought it was hilarious because he knew we were separated. I'm not sure whether he believed me. But one day I'll introduce you to him. He's half Italian like me.'

He was talking as though it was a given that she would stay with him. And yes, she would, but only on her terms. Little did he know that they didn't include a very vicious red head.

CHAPTER ELEVEN

DURING the meal Megan deliberately pushed all thoughts of Serena out of her mind, concentrating totally on Luigi. Not that it was difficult. In this cosy place, with its wooden walls and soft lighting, she felt that she was in a different world—a world where only the two of them existed. And she could do anything or be anybody she wanted.

'You're looking better.' His dark eyes, black in the low lighting, smiled into hers.

'I feel it,' she said. 'You were right about me being hungry. This Stroganoff is delicious.' She didn't really want to talk about food. It was what strangers talked about; food, the weather, particularly the weather. And Luigi was no stranger. Luigi was about to be seduced by his wife. The thought made her smile.

'And you certainly look happier.'

'It's strange there's no snow up here,' she said, not yet ready to let him know why she was feeling so happy.

'I'm glad because otherwise we mightn't have made it. There's been a heavy fall in Scotland, in the Aviemore area. Maybe we could go skiing while we're up here?'

'I've probably forgotten how to ski.' She hadn't done

any since the early days of their marriage when Luigi had taken her to Norway.

'Nonsense, it's like riding a bicycle. Once you've learned you never forget.'

Like making love with him. She had never forgotten how good it was. She might have told herself that she hated him, had even shut him out of her life for years, but at this moment in time she could recall every pleasurable moment they'd ever spent. It warmed her thinking about them; it set her toes curling in her shoes and her thighs pressing close together to try and stem the delicious flow of sensation that invaded her.

'I don't really think I want to go,' she said.

He grinned. 'Good, because I don't either. All I want to do is spend time here with you. This is the best place I know for rest and recuperation.'

Megan gave an inward smile. He wasn't going to get much rest.

'And we both have a lot of catching up to do.'

That was right.

'Lots to talk about.'

Hopefully actions would prove better than words.

'I want this to be a place where we sort out our problems.'

His problems!

'Where we start a new life together.'

Here! Here!

'Have you nothing to say about that?' he asked when she remained silent.

Megan smiled, a slow smile that lit up her entire face, not that she was aware of it. 'I think that perhaps tonight I'm too travel weary to talk. Let's just clear this stuff away and sit and listen to some music.' Romantic music preferably, seduction guaranteed.

'It suits me,' he said, jumping up from his chair immediately. 'I'll do the honours here, you fix the music. There are plenty of CDs to choose from.'

It made a change seeing Luigi in domestic mode and Megan quite enjoyed it. And he looked as though he was enjoying himself too. So what on earth had made him buy such a huge stark place for a home? A status symbol? That was all it could be. When they were back together—in every sense of the word, when she had ousted Serena, she would insist that they move.

They could have a large house without it being coldly impersonal. She didn't want to rattle around with a butler and cook and a whole retinue of servants. They could still employ Kate, and maybe a part-time housekeeper—they might need her if they had more children! Her thoughts had never got this far before but the idea appealed, and Charlotte would enjoy having a brother or sister to keep her company.

'Hey, you're supposed to be choosing music, not going into a daydream.'

Luigi had finished in the kitchen and had come to join her, and here she was, not a single CD selected, sitting on her haunches, staring into space.

'At least it must have been something good you were thinking because it's put a beautiful smile on your face. I was worried that you might not like it here, that you might miss Charlotte too much. Speaking of which, would you like to phone her before we settle down? There's no phone here but I've brought my mobile.'

How kind! Why had she ever felt that he thought more about work than he did her? Or was he intent on making the right impression? Would it last? During the next few days she had to make sure that it did. Make him want her so much that he would find it difficult to drag himself away, even for the few necessary hours he had to spend at work.

To her consternation there was no signal in the cabin, not even when she went outside and turned the phone every which way. She looked at Luigi in real concern. 'What if Kate needs to reach us? What if Charlotte suffers after-effects? What if something else happens to her?'

'I'm sure it won't,' he said, putting his arm about her shoulders. 'But don't get into a panic. I've already given Kate Michael's telephone number. If there's an emergency she'll ring the house and the message will be passed on to us.'

He had thought of everything, this man of hers. *This man of hers!* She liked that, it sounded good. He didn't belong to Serena any more. Not that he knew it at this moment, but at the end of their stay here he wouldn't even want to cast a glance in the other woman's direction. She would make sure of that.

It felt weird, planning to seduce her husband. Not that he would need much persuading, but she had to make very, very sure that his thoughts would never turn again to his gorgeous red-headed secretary. Not in the context of bedding her, at least.

'Come on, let's go back indoors,' he said gently. 'I don't want you catching cold.'

Megan hadn't realised quite how chilly it was until they were met by the warmth in the log cabin. She gave a huge shiver and went towards the fire with her hands outstretched.

'Shall we finish the wine or do you want a hot drink?' he asked.

'A huge mug of hot chocolate, I think,' she said. Then, realising that it wasn't in the least bit romantic, she changed her mind. 'No, let's finish the wine. You choose the music.' She sat down in a deep, comfortable armchair to one side of the fire and Luigi threw on another couple of logs, put on some CDs, poured their drinks, and then flopped into the chair opposite.

'I can't remember the last time I got away from everything like this,' he said, his head back, his eyes closed.

'You should do it more often. It's good for the soul.' Whatever that meant! She was able to study him unobserved and saw tired lines round his eyes and mouth that she'd never noticed before. He took on too much, *this man of hers*. Lord knew how many companies he owned these days, and he liked to have his finger on the pulse of every one. She would have to teach him differently. He had a few grey hairs at the temple as well, though she had to admit that she found them very attractive.

Suddenly she realised that his eyes weren't properly shut. He was studying her too from beneath lowered lids, and her body grew warm. She took a sip of her wine for courage then went over and sat on the floor beside him. He didn't say anything but she felt his surprise, and he stroked her hair as she rested her head on his thigh.

'This is nice,' he said, as Sibelius's *Finlandia* washed over them.

'Mmm.' She began stroking his thigh, tiny movements at first but then growing bolder, reaching higher, making each stroke more intense than the last, until he jerked away.

'Good God, woman, what are you trying to do to me?'

Megan smiled, a dreamy smile. 'Pardon? I wasn't doing anything, just listening to the music and—'

'Sending me to merry hell, you little witch.'

'Was I?' she asked with a frown. 'I'm sorry.' And she stood up and went back to her chair.

'Are you honestly trying to tell me that you didn't know what you were doing?' he growled.

'What *was* I doing?' It was hard trying to keep a look of innocence on her face. She wanted to laugh—and she wanted to do it again. She wanted to touch him, to feel the full force of his feelings for her. But she would save that for later. For the moment she wanted to tease him, to make him want her but deny him. She was being the *femme fatale*. A role she had never played before but one that she knew she would enjoy.

His eyes narrowed. 'It felt very much as though you were trying to arouse me. Not that that would be the case, of course, considering you've kept me at arm's length since Boxing Day.'

'You didn't like me sitting there?' she asked softly. 'It reminded me of when I was a child and I'd sometimes sit by my father while he read his newspaper. He'd absent-mindedly stroke my hair like you did.'

Dammit, he didn't want to be a father-figure. He wanted to be her husband, her lover, her heart's desire. He'd thought it was too good to be true when she came to sit by him. Megan wasn't in the habit of such arousing little gestures, not these days at any rate.

At one time, in the very early days of their marriage, she had loved to get him going. Sometimes coming up behind him and cupping her hands hard over his manhood, massaging expertly and sending him into instant readiness. Or she'd rub her breasts sensually against him, arching her body temptingly into his. She'd been everything a man could wish for—and he'd taken it all for granted!

Never again! If at the end of these few days he could manage to win her back he'd make sure he kept her for ever.

'Come here again,' he said softly. She did so but he thought it was reluctantly, and it saddened him. What had prompted her to sit by him in the first place? he wondered. Unless it was because she was worried about Charlotte? Maybe that was it, and she needed comfort.

This time she crossed her arms on his leg and resting her head on them, she stared into the flames licking up the chimney. 'It's so peaceful here,' she said.

'I'm glad you like it.'

'Why don't you buy a place like this?'

'If it will make you happy, then I will.'

'Not for me,' she said at once.

It felt like a rebuke. 'Why would I want such a retreat for myself?'

'I'm sure you could find someone to share it with.'

'There's no one I'd want except you.' He felt a sudden tension in her as he spoke. Perhaps now wasn't the time to insist. 'This is perfect, Megan. You and me. We can talk. We can relax. We can do whatever we like with no fear of interruptions. A far cry from my normal hectic schedule.'

'I can't believe you'd find this perfect,' she said. 'You thrive on being busy.'

It was true, he always had. It had taken the sudden jolt of finding out he had a daughter to bring him back to reality. And the discovery that he still loved his wife very much. He intended to do everything in his power to make sure she didn't run away again.

He hadn't liked threatening that he would take Charlotte away from her, and he wasn't even sure that he would have done, but at least it had done the trick. She was still here, and happy to be with him by the look of things. Unless, of course, she was simply humouring him? He prayed that she wasn't. He couldn't bear the thought of them spending three days together if she didn't really want to be here. He was hoping she would share his bed. If not tonight, then for the next two nights. It might take all his powers of persuasion, but that would be half the fun.

'I'm actually finding it a pleasant change,' he admitted quietly.

'For how long?' she asked. 'How long before you'll be itching to get back to the hub of things?'

'Oddly, I have no desire to do so. All I want is to be here with you, repairing our marriage.' As he spoke he stroked her hair again. Such soft, sweet-smelling hair. He wanted to bury his face in it; he wanted to bury his face in *her*. It was hard holding himself in check, stilling the desires that rose and raged.

Suddenly Megan lifted her face and looked at him, and in the glow from the fire he imagined that he saw love in her eyes. He was mistaken, of course, but just for a fraction of time she'd been the girl he had first met—the girl who had adored him from the start, and whom he'd loved deeply in return.

Silently he urged her to her feet and then encouraged her to sit on his lap, all the time expecting her to refuse, gladdened and excited when she eased herself down. *Finlandia* had changed into Frank Sinatra and as Megan rested her head on his shoulder and the old crooner serenaded them he felt that he was another step further towards his dream.

Poor Luigi. He didn't know what was going to hit him, thought Megan. He hadn't a clue that she was planning a concerted attack on his senses. He thought he had the upper hand; he thought he was the one taking the lead. He had no idea that she was in full control.

She began by blowing gently in his ear. It was something that had always turned her on, so why not him? And then she nuzzled his ear, then nibbled it. He tasted good, and he smelled wonderful. His breathing grew a little erratic but he didn't speak, or move, just a faint satisfied grunt in the back of his throat. As though he was waiting to see what she would do next.

You'd better be ready for it, mister, she said beneath her breath, because this is a full-scale sex attack. Actually, though, she hadn't quite thought about doing anything this early. She ought to at least have waited until tomorrow. 'Gosh, I'm sorry,' she said, drawing back. 'I can't think what came over me. It's a bit like old times, I suppose, and I forgot. You must be tired with all that driving. I expect you want to go to bed?'

'You mean you're going to stop?' he muttered thickly. 'Just when it was getting interesting? Unless, of course, you were suggesting we *both* went to bed?'

'I'm tired as well,' she admitted. Liar! She was wide-awake, and so aroused that it would be many hours yet before she was able to sleep.

'Then let's go up the wooden hill.'

'I didn't mean together,' she said, with a flash of false outrage in her eyes, getting up from his lap and glaring down at him. 'I'll take one of the beds down here. You can sleep upstairs.'

Luigi stopped breathing. This wasn't what he'd expected. He'd been sure that she was prepared to sleep with him. Well, almost sure. She had given all the right signs. Then he remembered to breathe again and dragged in a deep unsteady breath and pushed himself to his feet.

He wanted to question her. In fact he wanted to insist that she share the big bed upstairs, but a voice inside his head told him it would do no good. He had to play things her way if he wanted to get anywhere. And since she wasn't being coldly indifferent he could afford to be patient. So long as she didn't suggest the same arrangements every night!

'Whatever you like,' he said pleasantly, and caught a flicker in her eyes which told him that she'd been expecting him to object. 'I shouldn't have jumped to conclusions.'

'No, you shouldn't,' she returned, but she was smiling again. 'Goodnight, Luigi.' And she leaned towards him and kissed him full on the lips.

Megan smiled to herself as she felt Luigi's surprise, not even objecting when his arms imprisoned her and he deepened the kiss. She still planned on sleeping alone but meanwhile this could be a very pleasant night-cap. Or a highly erotic one!

He was probably feeling completely bewildered. One moment she was teasing him, the next declaring she was sleeping alone. That really had stunned him but he'd hidden his feelings well. Perhaps he'd learned his lesson. Realised that laying down the law got him nowhere at all. And perhaps pigs might fly! Luigi wasn't a man to give in. He'd declared that they needed to resolve their differences by talking. And they would talk, but little did he know that her plan was to evict Serena from his mind once and for all.

'Thank you for bringing me here,' she purred, rubbing her body gently against his, and then, just as his arms were about to close even tighter, she slid away from his embrace. 'Night, night, Luigi. Sweet dreams. See you in the morning.'

It was the sort of thing she said to Charlotte and she could tell by his clamped lips that he was aware of it. But she put an innocent smile on her face and skipped in the direction of the bedroom. It wasn't until she'd closed the door behind her that she realised her case was upstairs. Luigi had carried them both up earlier, evidently expecting her to sleep with him from the onset. His confidence sent a niggle of annoyance through her brain. For once she wanted to be in charge and it was infuriating to find that she was not.

Then came a tap on her door and it gently opened. Luigi appeared with a smile on his face and her bag in his hand. 'You forgot something.'

The fact that he was being so cheerful and understanding incensed her even further. 'So I did. Thank you.' And she virtually snatched it from him.

'Is there anything else that you require?'

'No, thank you.'

'There's plenty of hot water if you want a shower, or there's—'

'I said I'm OK.'

'I'll say goodnight then.' And still he stood there with that irritating smile on his lips.

'Goodnight, Luigi,' she said pointedly.

'You won't change your mind? It could get cold in the night, you know.'

'If I'm cold I'll come and crawl into your bed.'

'I'll be waiting.'

And you'll wait all night, she thought, as he finally closed the door. She was playing this game her way, not his.

Amazingly, as soon as she curled up beneath the duvet Megan fell asleep and when she woke the next morning a weak sun filtered in through a crack in the curtains. For just a moment she wondered where she was, then she sprang out of bed and looked eagerly through the window.

It had been too dark last night to see anything and now, to her delight, she saw that they were practically on the shore of a lake. Well, a hundred yards away, but that wasn't much. She spotted a path winding down to it—and there was Luigi making his way to the water's edge.

He had on a thick padded jacket pulled up to his ears and his hands were shoved deep into his pockets. Megan wanted to join him and wished he had woken her. She skipped through to the bathroom and then back to the bedroom and was soon dressed in her warmest clothes and running along the path he had taken.

Luigi turned and when she reached him he took her hands and looked deep into her eyes. 'I didn't expect you to be up this early. Did you sleep well?'

'Like a log. And you?' The hormones were buzzing again.

'Good,' he answered, but there were shadows beneath his eyes that hadn't been there last night.

'Why didn't you tell me we were this close to a lake?' she asked enthusiastically, turning away from him and taking everything in. With a backdrop of snow-capped mountains and a panorama of green fields and trees it was stunningly beautiful. Her eyes sparkled as she looked at him. 'It takes your breath away.'

'I knew you'd like it.'

'You *must* buy somewhere like this,' she said. 'I wish we'd brought Charlotte; she'd love it.'

'And you'd feel safe with her here with this vast expanse of open water? It makes my lake look like a puddle.'

'Perhaps you're right,' she agreed. But it was so incredibly lovely that it made her want to cry.

'Come on,' he said, with an arm around her shoulder. 'Let's get back indoors before we freeze to death. It looks as though we might have snow.'

There was an icy chill to the wind that she hadn't noticed till now, and the blue sky was already being taken over by ominous grey clouds.

Luigi kept his arm about her as they made their way to the cabin and it felt good. She even turned and gave him a peck on the cheek. Just that, nothing more, but his arm tightened and his brown eyes glowed like hot coals as he looked at her.

Indoors, Luigi cooked their breakfast while Megan laid the table. He must have lit the fire when he first got up, she decided, as flames and sparks shot spectacularly up the chimney. It was a perfect place to be; she couldn't have chosen anywhere better for her seduction of Luigi.

She sauntered through to the kitchen and stood in the doorway watching him deftly breaking eggs into the pan. 'You've become quite an expert,' she said lightly.

'It was either that after you left, or pile the weight on by eating out all the time.'

'I can't imagine you with even an ounce of extra fat,' she said, deliberately allowing her eyes to roam over the whole length of him. He wore a sky-blue polo shirt and close-fitting navy trousers that showed off his slim hips and taut behind, making her senses shudder into life. 'You've always had a superb body. And you certainly have none now. Did you stop exercising as well?' He'd been a gym fanatic at one time.

'I'm afraid so,' he admitted. 'Work took precedence. But—'

'But not any longer. I hope that's what you were going to say?' she suggested archly.

'Why would I want to work twenty-four seven when I have the most gorgeous wife in the world?'

Why would you want to bed another woman if that were true? Megan formed the question but didn't ask it. She had such faith in this holiday that it would break her heart if it didn't work. 'If you keep saying things like that,

and meaning them, then I think that perhaps we might
have a future.' She kept her eyes steady on his as she
spoke, unaware that they were shiny bright and she was
projecting an image of a woman falling in love again with
her husband.

His smile was warm and all enveloping and Megan felt
her breasts go taut beneath her lilac lambswool top, especially when his gaze dropped. It was one of her favourite
sweaters and she had teamed it with a pair of wide-legged
aubergine trousers. Luigi clearly approved because he
couldn't take his eyes away from her, until the eggs gave
a loud splutter and he turned just in time to rescue them.

'Perhaps I'd better move,' she said with a light laugh,
'or we'll be having burnt offerings for breakfast.'

'Perhaps I'd better kiss this ravishing wife of mine,' he
said, moving the pan off the heat and closing the space
between them. 'You look a million dollars this morning,
did you know that? The fresh air has brought an extra glow
to your cheeks. You look wonderful.'

The fact that he was taking the initiative when she had
planned to do the leading every step of the way escaped
Megan for the moment. She wanted this kiss, needed it like
a person dying of thirst, and her lips parted of their own free
will. Every pulse throbbed, blood coursed hotly through her
veins and she couldn't stop herself leaning into him, feeling
the same strident pounding inside Luigi as well.

'I think,' he said gruffly, 'that we should forget about
breakfast.'

So did she, but it wasn't part of her agenda. Sanity had
flickered briefly into her brain, telling her what she must
do. She gave the smile of an angel and pushed her hands
against his chest. The unsteady throb of his heart against
her palm felt like his life-blood pulsing into her, but she

bravely ignored it. 'Not on your life, I'm starving.' And she turned away from him.

She felt his shock and her lips twisted in amusement as she made her way towards the table. Not that she wasn't feeling deprived; that was an understatement. But she liked these little tasters of what was to come, and she prayed that Luigi liked them too.

There was silence in the kitchen for a few moments, before he spurred himself into action again. Megan sorely wanted to see his expression but knew that she dared not look round. Instead she sat down and poured them both a glass of orange juice, her back deliberately towards the door.

'Here we are.' He set down the coffee and teapots, a rack of toast, and finally her breakfast plate. It both looked and smelled delicious. Nicely crisp bacon, sausages, tomatoes, egg, fried bread. The perfect Full English Breakfast. It would be a miracle though if she ate it all.

She was hungry—she hadn't been lying when she said she was starving—but for one thing she didn't usually eat this much, and for another her hunger was turning into hunger for Luigi and not food. She was almost afraid to look at him now because she didn't want her feelings to be so blatantly obvious.

'I thought you were hungry,' he said, when she made no attempt to start.

'I am.' She eventually looked at him and saw not desire, as she'd expected, and which she knew would trigger off her own rampant mood, but concern.

'Perhaps I should feed you.' He cut a slice off his sausage and, picking it up with his fingers, he offered it to her.

With her eyes on his, Megan leaned slightly forward and opened her mouth. When he popped it in she felt the warm rasp of his fingers against her lips and she had an urge to suck them into her mouth too. But already he had moved and was preparing another morsel.

A tiny square of toasted bread this time, topped with golden egg. He was enjoying the game, feeding himself a mouthful in between times, until Megan took the initiative and began to feed him her breakfast in exactly the same manner.

It was the most erotic game they'd ever played, especially when fingers and food became intermingled, or when his eyes darkened with desperate need as she ran the tip of her tongue over her lips to collect any remaining crumbs.

Quite how they managed to finish the whole meal without leaving the table and making mad passionate love on the hearth she didn't know. There was a goatskin rug there and she'd had her eye on it ever since she'd arrived. It was where she intended to perfect her seduction routine.

'That was some breakfast,' he said when he had drunk two cups of coffee and she had finished what was left in the teapot.

'Perfect,' she announced. 'But far too much. I think that as soon as we've cleared away we should walk it off.'

He looked through the window. 'It's beginning to snow.'

And so it was, but nothing more than a few flurries.

'I can think of a much better form of exercise.' His face was straight but Megan knew exactly what he was talking about. The trouble was, he was beginning to take her for granted and this wasn't part of the deal she'd made with herself. Nothing had to come easy for him. He had to work for it, realise that some things were worth a bit of effort.

Like holding on to a wife whom he had taken for granted all those years ago!

CHAPTER TWELVE

MEGAN remained insistent that she wanted to walk, but by the time they'd stacked everything into the dishwasher and put on their outdoor clothes the snow was falling heavily. 'Shall we risk it?' she asked as they stood in the doorway watching the white flakes settle. Already it had coated the ground. 'If this keeps up it'll be inches deep within a few hours.'

'I'm game if you're game.'

'Then let's go,' she said with a laugh.

They trudged towards the lake, leaving footprints, Megan laughing when she slipped and Luigi's strong arms saved her. He held on fast to her after that, and the cold outside air that turned their breath into white mist was a huge contrast to the heat that raged inside her body.

When she slipped again, her feet going right from under her, Megan landed on her back. Luigi had released her for just a moment to point out a duck that was sheltering beneath some overhanging dead grasses, and now he knelt instantly beside her, real concern on his face. 'Megan, are you hurt?'

'Only inside.'

A deep frown gouged his brow. 'What do you mean?'

'It's something that only you can make better.'

'You know I'll do anything I can.'

'I want you to make love to me, Luigi, right here.' The words seemed to come of their own volition; they had nothing to do with her. She wasn't saying these things, it was crazy to want to make love in these freezing conditions.

There was a great silence around them. It was as though they were in the House of God. And, although she knew He wouldn't approve of an open-air ritual, it was what her heart desired.

'Are you sure?' There was the beginning of a smile playing on the edges of his mouth, and she could see that the idea had begun to appeal to him too.

Megan nodded.

'You're a crazy woman, do you know that? And you never fail to amaze me.'

She amazed herself too, if the truth were known.

Half expecting her request to fail because of how cold it was, Megan was exhilarated when Luigi performed with as much panache and aggressive eagerness as he'd ever done. Naturally they couldn't get fully undressed because of the still falling snow, but it was an experience to surpass all experiences.

And when it was over, when they'd both had time to draw breath, they ran laughing into the house ready to begin all over again. First of all they showered together in the spacious upstairs bathroom, turning it into a sensual game, each soaping the other, exploring each other's bodies, touching and kissing every sensitive zone.

Until Luigi exclaimed, 'Enough!' He insisted she stand while he towelled her dry, a long task because there were so many parts of her that needed different attention. Megan was sizzling by the time he'd finished touching and stroking and teasing and kissing.

He carried her to the bed and, although she was desperate again for him to make love to her, he refused to hurry. 'We have all the time in the world,' he told her gruffly.

So much for her being in charge! At this moment she was putty in his hands and he knew it. And he was making the most of it. Every single inch of her body was responsive to his touch, and she wriggled uncontrollably as he drew her to such a crescendo that she knew she would climax any second—without him!

It was only then that he entered her, slowly, only just controlling himself, and when Megan wrapped her legs around him and thrust her hips urgently upwards, he groaned and cursed and between them the world exploded.

'You're truly an incredible woman,' he said, once they'd come back down to earth. The covers were pulled over them and they were huddled together like two bunnies in a burrow. 'I thought I knew everything about you and yet you continue to surprise me.'

'I do?' she asked with a crooked smile.

'Since when has making love in the snow been an ambition of yours?'

She grinned. 'Never. It makes me shiver just thinking about it.'

'And yet you begged me for it. It was the most erotic thing I've ever done. I love you, Megan.'

His admission stunned her into stillness. 'Pardon?' she asked in the quietest of voices.

'I love you.' It was a simple admission, his tone suggesting that it was something he had always done and he couldn't understand why she was questioning him.

'Do you mean that?'

A faint frown narrowed eyes that were still dark with emotion. 'Of course I mean it. I've always loved you.'

'But you've never told me.'

'I know,' he admitted wryly, 'and I'm sorry. It's not something I find easy to do.'

'Because of your upbringing?'

He nodded, a shadow on his face as memories returned.

'So why tell me now? What's different?'

'The difference is *us*! I'm finally beginning to realise what a swine I've been. I'm keeping my promise to cut down on my workload. I'm putting family first. And since we came here things have changed as well. *You* are more relaxed. And I am more relaxed in your company. I find it easier to say what's in my heart.'

Megan felt as though all her hopes and wishes had come true at the same time, but she also knew that she still needed to exercise caution. This could be emotion speaking. In the cold light of day, when their bodies weren't entwined, when their senses weren't so heightened, he might feel differently.

'I think we should talk about this again later,' she said.

He frowned. 'You mean you don't believe me?'

'I want to.'

'But you don't!' he claimed roughly, rolling out of bed and glaring down at her. 'Dammit, Megan, what does a guy have to do to repair his marriage? Get down on my knees and beg? Believe me, that will never happen. You take me as I am or not at all.'

OK, if he wanted to get heavy then she'd let him have it. 'I don't want a husband who comes with baggage.' Her grey eyes glittered angrily and she too got up. But she didn't stand there naked as he was doing; she grabbed his robe and hugged it around her.

'Baggage? What the hell are you talking about?'

'As if you didn't know!'

'You mean Serena? For heaven's sake, Megan, when are you going to accept that there's nothing going on there?'

'That's not what she told me.' She saw the way his breath caught in his throat, the way his eyes stilled with suspicion, and she waited.

His words were slow and deliberate. 'You mean *Serena* told you—that she and I—were lovers? On New Year's Eve?'

Megan nodded.

He shook his head, unable to accept that she was telling him the truth. 'Why would she?' And it was clear to see that he didn't want to believe it.

'Because she's jealous, you blind idiot. She's in love with you.'

He winced then, giving away the fact that he'd suspected it. 'But I'm not in love with her.'

'That only makes a woman scorned more eager. Don't you know that?'

He ignored her question. 'And she actually came right out with it? She tried to make trouble between us?'

'Yes,' whispered Megan, finding it hard to see Luigi coming to terms with the fact that his PA was not as perfect as he'd thought.

'I don't suppose you want to tell me the details?'

And hurt him more? Megan shook her head.

'I've never taken her to bed.'

It was said so simply and sincerely that Megan accepted he was telling her the truth. She wouldn't have done a few days ago, but now she did.

'And I shall have a word with her when I go back to work. This won't happen again. She can stay in the job and behave, or leave.'

Megan's heart began to sing. 'I think I believe you this time, Luigi.'

She could see the relief flooding out of him, his body relaxing and a slow smile returning. 'I do love you, Megan, with all of my heart.'

'And I love you.'

'You'll stay with me for ever?'

She nodded.

He groaned and gathered her into his arms. 'I love you, I love you, I love you,' he claimed joyously. It was as though once he'd said the words, once he'd realised how easy it was to express his emotions, he couldn't stop.

'And I love you too. In fact I think we make a pretty good pair,' she added spontaneously.

'In bed and out of it,' he agreed, opening the robe she had folded protectively around her. When naked flesh met naked flesh their bodies set on fire, bed beckoned again and time lost all meaning.

Megan wasn't sure whether it was hours or days before they admitted hunger of a more prosaic kind. It seemed like for ever that they lay in bed pleasuring each other, sometimes reaching heights never before attained, sometimes dozing, their bodies still entwined. They had become one again in this peaceful place, and the next two days were filled with more of the same...

When it was eventually time for them to return home they were both sad. The car was packed, and they were taking a last look around to make sure they hadn't forgotten anything. 'I wish we could stay here for ever,' Megan said. 'Except that I'm missing Charlotte.' But not as much as she'd expected! Luigi had wiped everything from her mind. Her glorious husband.

'Me too, on both scores,' Luigi agreed firmly. 'I couldn't

have wished for a finer wife or a lovelier daughter, and I hope that one day in the not too distant future we shall have a brother or sister for her to play with.'

'I think that might happen sooner than you think,' Megan told him with an amazingly shy smile considering their uninhibited behaviour.

Luigi took her face between his palms, his eyes shocked and questioning. 'What are you telling me?'

'That I've missed my period.'

His eyes widened, like Charlotte's when she saw something wonderful. 'Which means that you could have conceived on Christmas Day? Or even Boxing Day?'

She nodded. 'Of course it could be that my system's out of sync because of all the upset I've had lately. It's a little early to tell, but—'

'But nothing!' he insisted. 'I knew there was something different about you. You have a bloom that only a pregnant woman has.'

'And how would you know what a pregnant woman looks like?' she taunted, and then wished she hadn't because she had deprived him of that opportunity with Charlotte.

But he didn't seem to mind. 'I love you, Mrs Costanzo. And I'm never going to stop telling you. And I love our daughter too, more than you'll ever know. I'm going to be the world's finest father—to all of our children.'

A spread of pleasure flooded Megan's limbs. She believed now in his reformation. Entirely.

'Charlotte got her daddy for Christmas,' he mused, 'and we created a new baby at Christmas. Isn't that just perfect?'

'Absolutely,' she said. 'And there's one thing I must do.'

He grinned. 'And that is? I'm not sure we have time to make love again.'

'I think I can manage to wait until we get home—just,'

she added with a provocative smile. 'But I need to tell my parents that we're back together. They thought the world of you, you know, and were really angry with me when I left. In fact, we haven't spoken since.'

'I know how they felt,' he agreed. 'I contacted them when I was trying to find you, and I promised I'd tell them if I ever did.'

'And did you?'

He nodded guiltily. 'They needed to know you were safe and well. I know I should have told you, but I still wasn't sure whether we'd make a go of things. You were so damn stubborn, so insistent that it was going to be a Christmas break and nothing more. I was terrified each time you threatened to leave.'

'What would you have done if I had gone?'

'Thought of a way to get you back. Believe me, my darling, I wasn't going to let you go again.'

'You won't have to worry now,' she said, secure in the knowledge that Luigi was going to be a perfect husband for all time. 'There's another couple of things, though.'

Luigi looked resigned. 'OK, spill them out. Let's not leave any skeletons in the cupboard.'

'It's nothing like that,' she assured him. 'Firstly, there never was anything going on between me and Jake. I let you think so to make you jealous. I'm sorry.'

'And you certainly did that,' he said. 'I hated the thought of any other man having you.'

'There's been no one but you,' she insisted.

He gave a pleased smile. 'So what's the other thing?'

Megan swallowed hard. 'Don't be hurt, but I don't like your house. Can we move?'

'Do you want to know the truth?' he asked with a sheepish grin. 'I don't like it either. At least, not since you've been living there. It's not a home, is it? It's too soulless. It doesn't have a heart. We'll choose something together, my darling, though it will have to be big enough to house all the children we're going to have.'

'Of course,' said Megan demurely.

He patted her tummy. 'Did I ever tell you that there are twins in my family?'

'Spare me, please,' she said with a laugh.

But actually the idea of having lots of babies for Luigi to dote on really appealed to her.

REQUEST YOUR FREE BOOKS!

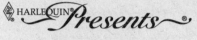

2 FREE NOVELS PLUS 2
FREE GIFTS!

YES! Please send me 2 FREE Harlequin Presents® novels and my 2 FREE gifts.
After receiving them, if I don't wish to receive any more books, I can return the shipping
statement marked "cancel." If I don't cancel, I will receive 6 brand-new novels every
month and be billed just $3.80 per book in the U.S., or $4.47 per book in Canada, plus
25¢ shipping and handling per book and applicable taxes, if any*. That's a savings of
close to 15% off the cover price! I understand that accepting the 2 free books and gifts
places me under no obligation to buy anything. I can always return a shipment and
cancel at any time. Even if I never buy another book from Harlequin, the two free books
and gifts are mine to keep forever.

106 HDN EEXK 306 HDN EEXV

Name	(PLEASE PRINT)	
Address		Apt. #
City	State/Prov.	Zip/Postal Code

Signature (if under 18, a parent or guardian must sign)

Mail to the **Harlequin Reader Service®**:
IN U.S.A.: P.O. Box 1867, Buffalo, NY 14240-1867
IN CANADA: P.O. Box 609, Fort Erie, Ontario L2A 5X3

Not valid to current Harlequin Presents subscribers.

Want to try two free books from another line?
Call 1-800-873-8635 or visit www.morefreebooks.com.

* Terms and prices subject to change without notice. NY residents add applicable sales tax.
Canadian residents will be charged applicable provincial taxes and GST. This offer is limited to
one order per household. All orders subject to approval. Credit or debit balances in a customer's
account(s) may be offset by any other outstanding balance owed by or to the customer. Please allow
4 to 6 weeks for delivery.

Your Privacy: Harlequin is committed to protecting your privacy. Our Privacy
Policy is available online at www.eHarlequin.com or upon request from the Reader
Service. From time to time we make our lists of customers available to reputable
firms who may have a product or service of interest to you. If you would
prefer we not share your name and address, please check here. ☐

INNOCENT MISTRESS, VIRGIN BRIDE

Wedded and bedded for the very first time

Classic romances from your favorite Harlequin Presents authors

Harriet Flint turns to smolderingly sexy Roan Zandros for a marriage of perfect convenience. But her new Greek husband expects a wedding night to remember... and to claim his inexperienced bride!

Meet the next Innocent Mistress, Virgin Bride in February 08:

ONE NIGHT IN HIS BED
by Christina Hollis
Book #2706

www.eHarlequin.com   HP12696

THE ROYAL HOUSE OF NIROLI

Always passionate, always proud.

**The richest royal family in the world—
a family united by blood and passion,
torn apart by deceit and desire.**

By royal decree, Harlequin Presents is delighted to bring you
The Royal House of Niroli. Step into the glamorous, enticing
world of the Nirolian Royal Family. The ailing king must find
an heir…each month an exciting new installment follows
the epic search for the true Nirolian king. Eight heirs, eight
passionate romances, eight fantastic stories!

BRIDE BY ROYAL APPOINTMENT
by Raye Morgan
Book #2691

Elena is drawn to Adam—the illegitimate child of a
Nirolian prince—and his little son, who's in need of
a mother…. But for Adam to marry her, he must put
aside his royal revenge.

***Don't miss the final installment of this fabulous
series, when the true heir shall be crowned!***

Coming in February:
A ROYAL BRIDE AT THE SHEIKH'S COMMAND
by Penny Jordan Book #2699